May 2019

Praise for THE BOLDS series

"This entertaining tale will make readers chortle.
A good choice for reluctant readers and fans of
Captain Underpants."

—*Booklist Online*

"In this humorously off-kilter tall tale . . . Clary mixes
animal fact with imaginative, entertaining fiction."
—*Publishers Weekly*

"[T]he tale avoids didacticism, delivering its message
of tolerance, inclusion, and kindness with irresistibly
quirky, anarchic glee. A winner of a sequel, just the
ticket for lovers of Roald Dahl."

—*Kirkus Reviews*

"This series sports the humor of Captain Underpants
and the heart of Winnie-the-Pooh. . . . A great choice
for any library collection serving kids."
—*School Library Journal*

Look out for other books
by Julian Clary & David Roberts:

The Bolds

The Bolds to the Rescue

The Bolds on Vacation

THE BOLDS
in Trouble

By Julian Clary

Illustrated by David Roberts

Carolrhoda Books • Minneapolis

First published in 2018 by Andersen Press Limited
First American edition published in 2019 by Carolrhoda Books
Published by arrangement with Andersen Press Limited

Text copyright © 2018 by Julian Clary
Illustrations copyright © 2018 by David Roberts

Carolrhoda Books
A division of Lerner Publishing Group, Inc.
241 First Avenue North
Minneapolis, MN 55401 USA

For reading levels and more information, look up this title at
www.lernerbooks.com.

Main body text set in Century Schoolbook regular 12.5/21.
Typeface provided by Monotype Typography.

Library of Congress Cataloging-in-Publication Data

The Cataloging-in-Publication Data for *The Bolds in Trouble* is on file at the
Library of Congress.
ISBN 978-1-5415-0045-7 (trade hardcover)
ISBN 978-1-5415-0047-1 (eb pdf)

Manufactured in the United States of America
1-43671-33484-7/23/2018

For Joshua

JC

In memory
of Mickeylove

DR

Chapter

Have you ever had something go wrong? You were expecting one thing and then something happened and you ended up getting something else completely different? Well, I have, and it can be most upsetting. My mother once made a chocolate cake for tea. I took a bite and spat it out. It tasted horrible!

"Don't be so silly," said my mother, rather crossly. "It's a lovely cake. Eat it!" But I couldn't bring myself to. So then she tasted it herself

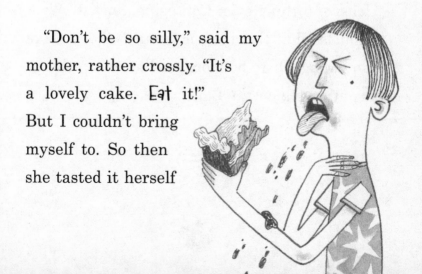

and she couldn't eat it either. "Something has gone wrong," she said, making a face and gulping down some water to take the awful taste away. Then she looked in the cupboard where she kept the ingredients. Do you know what she'd done? The cocoa powder was in a jar next to the gravy granules, and she'd mistakenly picked up the wrong jar. She'd made a gravy cake!

We've been laughing about that mix-up ever since. So you see, sometimes something funny happens by mistake. And sometimes what you think is going to be fun turns out to be the least fun thing ever. Confusing, isn't it? Well, that is what this book is about. When things go wrong. Or to be more precise, when things went wrong for the Bolds.

Life was as busy and eventful as ever in the Bolds' household.

The Bolds, as you probably know, are a family of hyenas living disguised as human beings on a pleasant tree-lined street called Fairfield Road in Teddington. They wear clothes and hats to cover their hyena features, and none of their human neighbors have guessed their secret, although they *have* noticed that the Bolds seem to laugh an awful lot. Being hyenas, they can't help themselves. They also like to rub their bottoms on tree trunks and bushes to mark their territory, but obviously they can't do that if anyone is watching.

Fred and Amelia Bold are the parents. Fred works at the Christmas cracker factory, writing the silly jokes, and Amelia makes and sells unusual hats at Teddington Market. Their children—twins Bobby and Betty— are lively and funny and sometimes a bit naughty. They go to the local school and are best friends with a girl called Minnie.

Minnie found out about the Bolds' secret a while ago but has promised to tell no one.

Next door lives Nigel McNumpty, who, as it turns out, is a grizzly bear. He was grumpy and lonely until the Bolds moved in, but now he's practically one of the

family. He has become best friends with Uncle Tony, an elderly hyena who the Bolds rescued from a local safari park along with Miranda, a sweet little marmoset monkey.

So that's everyone. Except it isn't quite. You see, the Bolds have gained a bit of a reputation for helping other members of the animal world who want to live like humans too. They take in all manner of waifs and strays, teach them how to walk and talk like humans, wear clothes, use a knife and fork, and even use the toilet. You'd be surprised how many animals there are living among us that we fail to notice aren't humans at all. Bus drivers, teachers, athletes, shop assistants . . . prime ministers, even. Only yesterday I had a new sofa delivered by two burly "men" wearing overalls. They huffed and puffed and snorted a lot, I noticed. It was only when I spotted their rather moist noses and saw a wisp of steamy sweat rising up in the air from their backs that I put two and two together. Yes, buffaloes. Brothers, I suspect. I didn't say anything. Buffaloes can be a bit bad-tempered, and I didn't want them to start pawing the ground and charging about. (Not with my new carpet and the collection of priceless porcelain dolls I've collected on my travels over the years.) But you see, I knew. And I knew because I have heard about the Bolds.

It wouldn't occur to most people to even think that animals were living in our midst, doing all manner of jobs and, it ought to be said, making an invaluable contribution to society.Only those clever people out there who have read the Bolds books will know to look. Won't we? Have a look around you now. Or if you're on your own, look out the window. Or if it's dark, turn on the TV. There's one particular news anchor who has all the characteristics of a turtle. Actually, no, don't do that. Reading is much better for you than watching TV. And there's nothing much on these days, is there? But next time you're out and about, see how many "people" you can spot who you suspect are animals in disguise. Your teacher perhaps? The bus driver? Or maybe the lady who works in the candy store?

Probably best not to tell them you've figured it out, though. Just give them a knowing look and tap the side of your nose.

But anyway, where was I? Ah yes, the Bolds' household. That's all the permanent residents accounted for. But, as I've explained, the Bolds sometimes teach and help animals to make the transition to the human way of life. So when this story begins, there were a few other guests at 41 Fairfield Road whom I really ought to tell you about. The current crop of live-in students at the

Bolds' included a wild boar called Craig, who had trotted all the way to Teddington from a field in Newbury (Craig's ambition was to start

his own brewery selling delicious homemade truffle-flavored alcohol-free beer); Miss Paulina the otter, who didn't have a career in mind but thought she might have a vocation as a nun; and a very noisy,

rather argumentative goose called Snappy, who would one day make a very good traffic warden.

Let's get going. Our story begins with a series of mysterious disappearances. Things start to go missing, and what this leads to is a whole heap of trouble for the Bolds.

One summer day, before lunchtime, Bobby Bold decided to make himself a cheese sandwich. He buttered two thick slices of bread, piled some cheese and pickles on one, slapped the other slice on top, cut it in half, and put it on a plate.

"What else?" he thought. "Ah, a nice tomato would be tasty." He turned around to get one from a bowl on the other kitchen counter, rinsed it under the tap, and turned back to his sandwich. But would you believe it? The sandwich was gone. Vanished. Just a few crumbs left. He blinked at the empty plate, looked to the left and the right in case he'd moved it, looked over to where the tomatoes were, but there was no sign of the cheese sandwich anywhere. Bobby scratched his head and frowned. Had he eaten it and forgotten? His stomach rumbled loudly, so he knew that wasn't it. He looked around again, even opening the fridge and peering inside, just in case he'd put it there.

Some people might have gotten mad at this point, but Bobby hardly ever got mad. He wasn't the type. In fact, he smiled.

"Someone is playing a game with me!" he said to himself. "Very funny!" He folded his arms and laughed. "I know it's you, Betty!" he shouted. "You can come out now." But there was no reply. So he opened all the cupboards, fully expecting to find his mischievous twin sister hiding there, but with no results.

"Aha!" he said at last, noticing the back door was open. Bobby wandered into the backyard, where Uncle Tony was snoozing in a deck chair and his sister Betty was standing on the patio with her hands on her hips looking angrier than usual.

"Did you drink my lemonade?" she accused her brother. "I just put it here while I went to get my book, and now it's all gone."

Bobby gasped. "No way. I was inside making a sandwich, which has also disappeared."

"Well, if it wasn't you, who was it? The only

other person around is Uncle Tony." The twins looked over to the elderly hyena, dozing in his chair on the lawn.

"He certainly loves sandwiches and lemonade," agreed Bobby. "And he's got crumbs on his T-shirt," he said, getting a little closer.

"He's always got crumbs on his T-shirt," pointed out Betty, "but I'm pretty sure he's faking that snoring."

"Yes, nice one, Tony," said Bobby. "You had us going there for a minute."

But Uncle Tony was deaf as a post these days, and he didn't respond. In fact, he was snoring quite loudly and appeared to be fast asleep. His mouth was wide open.

"Ha ha!" laughed Bobby. "He looks so innocent." But he was sure Uncle Tony had crept in and taken his sandwich. "Let's see how fast asleep you really are, shall we?" he chuckled.

"What are you going to do?" asked Betty.

"Wait and see!" said Bobby, laughing wildly
as only a hyena can.

Chapter

2

Bobby returned to the kitchen and got a squeezy bottle of mustard from the fridge. He crept back to Uncle Tony, opened the lid, held the mustard upside down over the hyena's open jaws, and squeezed: a big dollop of hot mustard drooped down from the bottle like a giant yellow dewdrop. Bobby gave another gentle squeeze.

The dollop trembled for a second before falling silently into Uncle Tony's mouth.

Then Bobby and Betty darted behind a shrub to watch the fun.

At first nothing happened. Then the snoring stopped abruptly and Uncle Tony's nose twitched and his mouth slowly closed.

It occurred to Bobby that, for someone pretending to be asleep, Uncle Tony was being very convincing. Oh dear, what if he *wasn't* the one who'd stolen the sandwich? But it was too late now . . .

Suddenly Uncle Tony's eyes opened. Just a little at first, then wider, wider, and WIDER! At the same time, he made a few gentle throat-clearing noises, which quickly gathered momentum until he was coughing and wheezing rather loudly. Eventually a spray of yellow saliva flew across the lawn, and poor Uncle Tony staggered out of his deck chair, his eyes streaming and his nose running as he pawed frantically at his mouth, trying to stop the burning taste. Unable to see properly, he ended up on his arthritic knees crawling, choking, and gasping all at once, trying to call for help.

From behind their shrub Betty and Bobby could see that this "joke" had not been funny at all and had actually gone dangerously wrong. They rushed out to help.

"It's all right, Tony!" shouted Betty, running to turn on the hose. "Open your mouth and I'll wash it away. Open wide!" She directed the jet of water into Tony's open snout, but the poor hyena wasn't expecting that either and hadn't closed his throat. The water went down the wrong pipe and only made matters worse. Now he was coughing and gasping for air too.

Hearing the commotion, Mrs. Bold rushed out of the house. "What on earth are you doing to Tony?" she demanded. She grabbed the hose from her daughter and threw it to one side.

"Tony, Tony!" she said, putting her arm around him and leading him back to the deck chair. "Just stay calm and try to breathe."

"W-w-we thought he was playing tricks on us!" said Bobby, ashamed. "Oh dear. Is he going to be all right?"

"Get him a glass of water, quickly! And a towel!" said Mrs. Bold. Her children ran into the house to do as they were told.

Slowly Uncle Tony recovered, but he was soaking wet, was bewildered, and had rivulets of hot yellow stuff running down his face and chest. Mrs. Bold wiped his aged gray fur with her apron and coaxed him into drinking a few sips of water.

"There, there," she said gently. "You're all right now, Tony. Calm yourself."

"Oh my," said Tony, his voice shaking. "I was having a lovely nap one minute, then suddenly my mouth was on fire, and it felt like I was underwater. What on earth happened to me?" He peered at Mrs. Bold full of bewilderment. "Was it a bad dream, Amelia?"

"I honestly don't know," said Mrs. Bold. Then she turned to her sheepish-looking children. "Do you two know what happened?"

"I, well, yes . . ." began Betty.

"We thought he was only pretending to be asleep, that he'd stolen my sandwich and Betty's drink as a joke, so I, er, I—"

"You what?" asked their mother, frowning

as she picked up the half-empty bottle of mustard.

"Put mustard in his mouth," said Bobby awkwardly. "It was supposed to be funny. I'm sorry, Tony, really I am."

"Well, it wasn't funny, was it?" said Mrs. Bold. "In fact, it was terribly un-funny. I'm surprised at you, Bobby. I really am. And you, Betty. Doing something that unkind to an elderly family member."

Uncle Tony looked up at the twins, bleary-eyed and a little confused. "You didn't mean to hurt me. I know you'd never do that. It was a joke that went wrong, that's all. When I was a pup in the wild, I used to think it was great fun to chase my own tail. Then I caught it one day and bit it. Made myself yelp with pain. It wasn't funny anymore and I never did that again. I guess this is a similar thing."

"Except the children aren't living in the wild," sniffed Amelia. "Although they act like it sometimes."

Mr. Bold suddenly appeared at the back door. "What's going on here? Pups chasing tails? I've got a joke about that."

Why did the pup chase his tail?

He was trying to make ends meet!

Mrs. Bold giggled, although she was trying to be firm with the children.

What do you do if a pup eats a dictionary?

Take the words out of his mouth!

Uncle Tony liked this joke and let out a loud, rather croaky guffaw.

How do you tell the difference between a pup and a marine biologist?

One wags a tail, the other tags a whale!

By now everyone was laughing. The unfortunate incident with the mustard was explained to Mr. Bold and then quickly forgotten as the hyenas did what hyenas do best: laughed long and loud until they were all rolling around on their backs on the lawn.

It was some minutes later, during a pause in the hilarity, that a sudden pang of hunger reminded Bobby of something.

"What I don't understand, though," he said, sitting up and scratching his head, "is where my sandwich went."

There was a puzzled silence as all of them pondered this cheesy mystery.

"Well, it wasn't any of us," shrugged Mrs. Bold. "Miranda?"

Uncle Tony shook his head. "She's fast asleep inside my T-shirt." Just then a sleepy marmoset monkey popped her head out into the open air.

"What happen? Me dream me on boat. Big storm. Thunderclaps!"

"That was me coughing. Sorry!" said Uncle Tony.

"Ah, poor Tony!" squeaked Miranda. "You no got coff-coffy?"

"No, my sweet. Just a, er, misunderstanding involving some hot mustard."

"No coff-coffy no more. Nighty nighty!" said Miranda as she gave a yawn and retreated back inside Uncle Tony's T-shirt to continue her siesta.

"Perhaps it was Mr. McNumpty who took my sandwich?" pondered Bobby next, glancing over the fence.

"No. He's gone to the library, I believe," said his father. "He's heard there's a book about a bear called Winnie who does a poo somewhere. Something like that anyway."

"And frankly, he's a bit too big to creep in unnoticed and silently snatch your lunch," pointed out Mrs. Bold.

"Mind if I go back to sleep?" asked Tony, his eyes beginning to droop.

"Of course not, old boy," said Mr. Bold, giving the elderly hyena a pat on the shoulder. "And the children are very sorry for the mustard business, aren't you?"

The children nodded.

"All forgotten," said Uncle Tony.

What's huge and gray and sends people to sleep?

A hypno-potamus!

But Uncle Tony didn't hear the punch line. He was fast asleep.

Chapter

The Bolds all wandered back into the house.

"Oh well. I guess we'll never know what happened to that sandwich," said Bobby. "Can I make another one?"

"Certainly," said his mother. "Though I think I know who might have taken the first one."

"Who?" asked her family.

"Well, Craig, Miss Paulina, and Snappy are in the front room with the dress-up box, learning about clothes and how to wear them.

Maybe one of *them* got hungry and took your sandwich? They haven't had their manners lessons yet, so perhaps they don't know it's wrong to take things without asking."

In the front room the three students were indeed coming to terms with the tricky business of dressing themselves. It's not as easy as it looks when you haven't done it before and you haven't had a parent or helper to teach you *how* to do it.

Craig the wild boar had squeezed his big barrel chest into a slim-fit coral pink shirt, and several of the buttons had burst under the strain. He had a pair of trousers on, but they were inside out and back to front.

Miss Paulina, the religious otter, had made herself a sort of wimple out of a pair of pastel green shorts—her face was peeking out of one

leg and her hindquarters somehow out of the other. Her ensemble was finished off with a pair of white tennis shoes, the laces of which were still tied together, causing her to fall over, and she lay wriggling on her back trying to get upright again, her big otter tail swishing about frantically.

As for Snappy the goose—well, he'd clearly been pecking furiously at every item he could reach and was sitting in a torn, tattered nest of fabric while other scraps, threads, and fragments floated down around him like confetti.

The Bolds entered the living room and tried not to laugh at the chaotic scene, but they couldn't help themselves.

"Er, how are you all doing?" asked Mrs. Bold, covering her snout with both paws.

"I don't think we've quite got the hang of things," huffed Craig.

"No. You're all . . . pants!" quipped Mr. Bold.

"Clothes are stupid, in my opinion," snapped Snappy. "Feathers are far more sensible."

"But humans wear clothes, so you'll have to persevere," said Mrs. Bold.

"I'll help you," offered Betty.

"Practice makes perfect," said Miss Paulina with a virtuous smile.

"A good first attempt," said Mr. Bold. "Now, do any of you know anything about a missing sandwich?" he asked as he and his family helped the students out of what was left of their clothes. "Bobby made one and then it vanished into thin air before he had a chance to eat it."

Snappy turned and glared at the Bolds, his beak wide with disbelief. "Are you calling us thieves?" he said, his long neck jutting forward accusingly. "The nerve!"

"No, we, er, just wondered, only—"

"Wondered if we accidentally stole a sandwich? I've never been so insulted in all my days!"

"Please don't get upset, Snappy!" said Bobby. "We were just trying to solve the mystery."

"No sandwiches have been eaten by us, unfortunately," said

Craig, patting his stomach.

"We are innocent of all charges," added Miss Paulina, nodding in agreement. "But I will pray for the safe return of your missing lunch."

The Bolds left them to it and went to the kitchen, where they began making sandwiches for everyone.

As Mr. Bold was slicing the cheese, his wife suddenly gripped his arm and sniffed the air.

"I've got it!" she said triumphantly.

"Got what? My sandwich?" asked a confused Bobby.

"No. The culprit. I know who the sandwich thief is! I can smell him!"

Mr. Bold put the knife down and sniffed the air too, taking several big, noisy lungfuls.

"Aha!" he said. "Me too!"

And together they said,

We smell
FOX!

Chapter

The Bolds' animal instincts were right. It was indeed a fox who had stolen the sandwich and lemonade, before helping himself to a couple of homemade cupcakes left cooling in the kitchen at Number 45. He then jumped over the fence and took three old steak bones, which he found in the garbage at Number 47. But his daylight raids on the houses of Fairfield Road had not gone unnoticed, and there was trouble brewing on that quiet, tree-lined street.

A few hours later, Tony was awake after his rest, and the twins' best friend, Minnie, had popped over with her little dog, Walter.

Everyone was sitting around the kitchen table enjoying some cookies and lemonade, when there was a polite tap on the back door.

"Who's there?" said Mr. Bold.

"Rita," replied a deep voice.

"Rita who?"

"Rita lot of books!" said the deep voice again. Then Mr. McNumpty entered, carrying a big pile of books from Teddington Library.

"Ha ha!" said Mr. Bold. "That's a good joke. I must remember that and use it in a cracker."

"Would you like some lemonade and a cookie?" asked Mrs. Bold.

"Oh, yes, please!" said Mr. McNumpty, putting the books on the counter before washing his hands in the kitchen sink.

Once they were all settled and happily chomping on some homemade cookies, the Bolds told their neighbor about the missing cheese sandwich and lemonade and the joke with the mustard that had gone horribly wrong.

"And then we discovered who the real thief was," said Mrs. Bold. "Bet you can't guess who."

"Ah, well, maybe I can," teased Nigel. "Was it a fox?"

"How did *you* know?" said Mrs. Bold.

"Because I saw one of these in the library," said Mr. McNumpty, pulling a leaflet from his jacket pocket. Betty immediately picked it up and started reading:

ATTENTION

Fairfield Road Residents' Association is calling a meeting tonight at Number 10 Fairfield Road to discuss the alarming problem of urban foxes in our area.

Foxes are entering our homes and yards day and night in search of food. Something must be done to rid us of these wild, disease-ridden vermin before the problem gets more serious and someone is hurt.

Please come along at 7 p.m. sharp. Soft drinks and snacks will be provided.

Richard and Zoe Bingham
10 Fairfield Road

"Gosh," said Mr. Bold. "I don't think the poor foxes are dangerous! Unless you're a cheese sandwich."

"And I don't think they're disease-ridden, either!" said Mrs. Bold indignantly. "Why do humans always assume that animals are carrying diseases?"

"I don't," pointed out Minnie. "You're the cleanest, loveliest friends in the world."

"Thanks," said Betty. "I just don't understand why people think the fox will hurt them. Surely it's the other way around. My teacher says that in the old days people used to hunt foxes."

"Yes," said Minnie. "And there's a stuffed fox in the café on Broad Street. I saw it when we went out for Mom's birthday. It had glass eyes and a really sad face."

Mrs. Bold shuddered. "Sometimes I really don't understand human beings. How cruel! Surely that's far worse than a fox who steals the odd sandwich."

"When we lived in Africa," said Mr. Bold, "your mother and I were always scavenging in the safari park."

"Fred . . ." Mrs. Bold gave him a warning look.

"Well, it's true, my dear. It's what hyenas are famous for—and laughing, of course."

"We've left that life behind us now," Mrs. Bold reminded him.

"Yes, I know, but it doesn't mean I'm not sometimes tempted by the delicious smells coming out of garbage cans."

Betty and Bobby giggled—and Minnie pushed her cookie away, looking a little queasy.

"What I mean," continued Mr. Bold, "is that I would never condemn an animal for doing what comes naturally to it."

"But the Binghams seem very upset about the foxes' natural behavior," said Minnie.

"They seem to be upset most of the time," pointed out Mr. McNumpty.

The Binghams were known to everyone on Fairfield Road as busybodies. They were a retired couple who seemed to spend most of their (considerable) spare time watching everyone else on the street to make sure they didn't do anything they considered "wrong." If your car wasn't parked neatly, they put a note on your windshield. If children played on the street outside their house, they knocked on the window. And if you didn't trim your hedge, they put a terse letter under your door.

"I think we need to go to this meeting and stick up for the foxes," said Mr. Bold. "Goodness knows what the Binghams are proposing to do about the 'problem,' but I think it's our duty to defend the poor creatures and remind people that animals are not the dangerous ones around here. Why, only yesterday I saw a poor pigeon as flat as a pancake lying in the gutter where it had been squashed by a car. Surely careless driving is far more dangerous than a hungry fox who occasionally helps himself to a snack."

"Speaking of snacks, I wonder what the snacks will be at this meeting," pondered Bobby, licking his lips.

"I don't know," said his mother, "but *you* won't be trying any. You'll be in bed."

"Cheesy balls?" said Bobby.

"I beg your pardon?"

"Do you think there'll be cheesy balls? I love them!"

"Then you'll love my new cheese jokes," said Mr. Bold.

"I've got one!" said Bobby, who had inherited his father's love of jokes.

"Go on then, son!" said Mr. Bold proudly.

"I know!" jumped in Mr. Bold.

"Halloumi!"

Everyone was enjoying the cheesy jokes and had almost forgotten about the foxes.

"It's such fun to have a jolly good laugh," said Uncle Tony, wiping tears from his bristly cheeks.

"The best things in life are Brie!" said Mr. Bold.

Chapter

So that evening Mrs. Bold brushed her ears and put on a nice hat, and Mr. Bold checked himself for fleas while Uncle Tony got Betty and Bobby ready for bed. Then when the twins were tucked in, their parents went next door to call for Mr. McNumpty.

"Now remember," said their neighbor, "we need to defend these poor foxes without arousing the local residents' suspicions to the fact that we too are animals. A lovely hat, by the way, Amelia—it covers your ears beautifully."

"Why, thank you," said Mrs. Bold, blushing a little. "I've gone for a smart but casual look."

When they arrived at Number 10, they found the house positively bursting. Another neighbor opened the door to them because Mr. Bingham was busy trying to find more chairs, and Mrs. Bingham was repeating for the *sixth* time the terrifying story of finding a fox peering in through her French windows.

"And I said to myself, there and then, 'Zoe Bingham, it's up to you to do something about this problem before someone really gets hurt.'"

The Bolds and Mr. McNumpty were ushered into the front room. Mrs. Bold found a stool to sit on, but Mr. Bold and Mr. McNumpty had to stand at the back. Mr. Bold looked around for the promised snacks but was rather disappointed: just a single bowl of chips of indeterminate

flavor and some rubbery carrot sticks with a beige dip that might have been hummus (but not from one of the better supermarkets) served on a chipped platter. Furthermore, the meeting was so well attended, these sparse offerings were gobbled up in no time. Mr. Bold thought about licking the bowl the chips had been in but decided he'd better not and made do with his watery glass of lemonade. But the poor quality of the refreshments was soon forgotten once the heated debate got under way.

"Foxes are everywhere. We must do something!" declared Mr. Bingham ominously, before Mrs. Bingham told again the story of the fox peering in at her French windows.

And the rest of the neighbors seemed to be in agreement that the foxes were a nuisance.

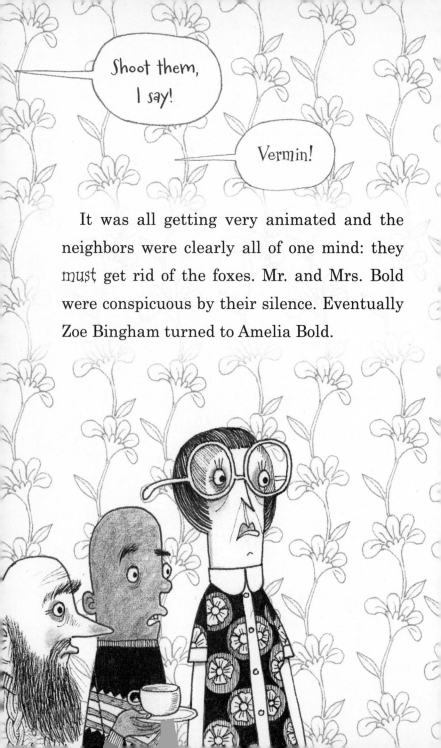

It was all getting very animated and the neighbors were clearly all of one mind: they must get rid of the foxes. Mr. and Mrs. Bold were conspicuous by their silence. Eventually Zoe Bingham turned to Amelia Bold.

"Well, what do *you* think? Have you been invaded yet?"

"Well, I rather like foxes," said Mrs. Bold.

The room suddenly fell silent.

"You like them?!"

"Er, yes. Beautiful creatures," continued Amelia. "And I don't see why we can't all get along together perfectly well."

There was a collective gasp. Mrs. Bold looked to her husband for support. Mr. Bold looked rather blank for a moment, and then his eyes lit up.

What did the grape say when the fox stepped on it?

Nothing. He just let out a little wine!

Several neighbors tutted disapprovingly and exchanged glances with each other.

"My husband works in the Christmas cracker factory," explained Mrs. Bold. "He writes the jokes . . ."

"Good for him," sniffed Richard Bingham. "But I find it hard to believe that your house is the only one that hasn't been affected by these wretched foxes. Something must be done!"

"Well, there are natural ways to deter foxes," said Mrs. Bold.

"Yes," said Mr. McNumpty. "I read in the library that they don't like male urine. Perhaps you could pee around your yard to stop the foxes coming in."

"Do what around our yard?" fumed Mr. Bingham. "I've never heard anything so disgusting."

"Lion poop," shouted someone else.

"I beg your pardon?"

"Lion poop. Apparently foxes hate lion poop. Let's get some of that."

(That's actually true, by the way. I know it sounds crazy, but look it up if you don't believe me!)

"Where on earth are we going to get lion poop from?" laughed Mrs. Bingham in an unpleasant way. "This is Teddington, not Africa."

"You could try London Zoo," suggested Mr. Bold.

Mrs. Bingham shuddered. "Really. If that's

the best solution you can come up with, then I think it's probably better if you keep your solutions to yourself. We need to get rid of these foxes—we're not going to achieve that by peeing and pooping in our backyards!"

"Animals and humans can live together perfectly well, so long as we are considerate and respectful," stated Mr. McNumpty. "I expect the foxes have lived here a lot longer than we have."

"But they should live in the countryside. Not here in Teddington."

"Why should they?" said Mr. McNumpty. "Who says?"

"I say!" said Richard Bingham, getting rather red in the face.

This set everyone off again, and the room was very soon in an uproar.

Mrs. Bold and Mr. McNumpty tried to argue that *no* children had been bitten, nor would they be, and that foxes are generally clean animals. But no one could hear them. Mr. Bold had several more foxy jokes up his sleeve, but *he* couldn't be heard either.

In the end there was nothing Mr. and Mrs. Bold or Mr. McNumpty could say to change anyone's opinion, and it was decided that a private pest control company called Pow to Pests! should be contacted. They would catch the foxes in a trap and then drive them out to the middle of nowhere and let them go.

"But won't they just find their way back?" asked one lady. "My dog found his way back from Guildford when we left him at my mother's."

"Well, that's why I'm suggesting we use Pow," said Mr. Bingham. "I have it on good authority (although they'll never admit it) that the foxes aren't really 'let go.' They're 'dealt with' in the countryside."

"What do you mean?" asked Mrs. Bold.

"I mean they go to fox heaven!"

Mrs. Bold looked confused.

"They kill them," said Mrs. Bingham bluntly. "In a very humane way," she added. "I don't suppose they feel a thing."

"Well, we don't know that for certain," said Mr. Bingham. "But suffice to say this company gives a one hundred percent guarantee that the foxes won't return."

"But that's murder," said Mr. Bold. "You can't do that."

"We can and we will. All those in favor of using Pow to rid us of this problem, raise your hands."

Every hand in the room went up, except the paws of Mr. Bold, Mrs. Bold, and Mr. McNumpty.

Chapter

By the time they got home, Mrs. Bold was crying and Mr. Bold had lost the desire to tell any jokes.

"Oh dear," said Uncle Tony when he saw everyone's faces. "It didn't go well, then?"

"It was awful," said Mrs. Bold, blowing her snout loudly into a handkerchief. "They want to catch those poor foxes in a cage and take them away . . ."

"To be killed," added Mr. McNumpty.

"Oh, poor foxy!" cried Miranda. "They no deservey that."

"I know," agreed Mr. Bold. He was feeling rather guilty. "I have to admit I've been down the odd garbage bin myself when no one was looking. Found half a pizza the other week in the one at Number 15. I could smell it from here. Still warm, it was!"

"It would have been a terrible waste. You did the right thing," agreed Uncle Tony.

"But now a fox has probably gotten the blame," said Bobby, who was listening at the door with his sister.

"What are you two doing up?" asked his mother.

"We couldn't sleep. We wanted to hear about the meeting."

"Well, it's not something I want you hearing about."

"Too late, Mom, we've already heard. The foxes are in grave danger."

"We've got to do something," said Betty.

"We warn foxy!" piped up Miranda from her spot on the windowsill. "Tell foxy be careful. Peeps out to get them!"

"That," said Mr. Bold, "is an excellent idea, Miranda."

"You welcome," said Miranda.

"We can speak to the foxes, animal to animal, and tell them the danger they're facing. But we'd better act quickly. The pest control van will probably be here tomorrow. Those Binghams don't want to waste any time," added Mrs. Bold.

"But how do we contact the foxes?" asked Bobby.

"We go to Bushy Park," said Uncle Tony. "I've definitely smelled fox when I've taken a stroll through the park. There's a distinct aroma near the ice cream van. If those ones aren't the culprits, we can at least get a message to them through one of their clan."

"Right," said Mr. Bold, looking at the clock on the mantel. "The park. Of course. It's nearly nine o'clock now. It will soon be getting dark . . ."

"Foxy come out at dusk," offered Miranda.

"Or any time they're hungry," corrected Bobby. "It was just before lunchtime when my sandwich went missing."

"We need to be careful, though," warned Mr. McNumpty. "If our neighbors see us having a cheery chat with a fox, their suspicions will be aroused. The last thing we need is people suspecting we're animals and capturing us too."

"Very true," said Uncle Tony. "Very true."

"This will have to be an undercover operation," concluded Mr. McNumpty. "We will have to creep into the park at midnight, once everyone else is safely tucked in bed."

"That's rather late for the twins," cautioned Mrs. Bold.

"Please let us come," said Betty. "We promise to be good."

"Come on, Dad," said Bobby. "We've been on all your adventures before. We won't be able to sleep anyway, knowing you're out there trying to help other animals."

"What do you think, Fred?" said Mrs. Bold.

"Well, this is an emergency. The future of these foxes is at stake. I think under the circumstances we'd better let the twins come with us."

"Very well, Bobby and Betty," said Mrs. Bold. "You may come too. It's Sunday tomorrow, so at least you'll be able to sleep in."

What nice parents animals are. Most human parents would have said, "Absolutely not. Wandering around the park at midnight? No way. Go to bed." Bobby and Betty were very lucky pups.

"There's just one problem," said Mr. McNumpty, rubbing his chin. "The park is closed at night. The gates will be locked."

"Hmmm," said Mr. Bold. "Hadn't thought of that."

"Well," reasoned Bobby. "If the foxes can get out, we must be able to get in."

"Maybe there's a hole?" suggested Mrs. Bold. "We'll find a way through, I'm sure."

"Could we dig?" suggested Betty.

"Or take the students with us," said Bobby. "*They* could help. Craig is very strong, and Miss Paulina has sharp teeth."

"I don't think so," said Mrs. Bold. "They're not ready for such a serious excursion. They still can't dress themselves, and they might give us away. Leave them here asleep."

"Come on then, let's all try to get a little sleep before our mission begins," said Mr. Bold. "We will leave for the park at midnight. These foxes need our help. We'll find a way in."

Chapter

7

So later that night, when all the lights in all the houses on Fairfield Road were out, the Bold family and Mr. McNumpty quietly left Number 41 and crept along to the gates of Bushy Park.

But how were they going to get over the wall? There was no sign of a hole. It looked like they would have to start digging, which Mr. Bold worried would take too long and might alert someone to what they were doing. But as it happens, Mrs. Bold had rather cleverly decided to wear one of her unusual hats, and this one was made of old bed springs, just in case they were needed. And of course they were.

"My dear, you're a *genius!*" declared Mr. Bold. "We'll tie them to our feet and bounce over the wall!" And so they did—one by one. There were some mishaps, of course, where they didn't quite bounce high enough and hit the wall, but after much stifled laughter and some trial and error, the whole party finally made it into the park.

It was pitch black, but luckily, hyenas can see in the dark.

"This way," said Betty. "Follow me." And she led the others to an area of the park that was quite wild and overgrown with brambles and ferns.

"They should be around here somewhere," she said, peering into the darkness. They all waited for a while, but there was only silence and the odd hoot of an owl watching from the trees above.

Then Mr. McNumpty spotted two sly eyes peering at them from several yards away.

"Yoo hoo!" he called. "Mr. Fox? Mrs. Fox? Do you think we might have a word? It's rather urgent. Don't worry, we're not really humans. We're animals in disguise. I'm actually a grizzly bear and my friends here are hyenas."

Now you might think it unlikely that a

grizzly bear could speak to a fox and expect any kind of answer, but there is a simple explanation: all animals can understand each other. What sounds to us like incomprehensible barks, growls, purrs, or squawks are all crystal clear if you're an animal, of whatever species. Therefore a zebra can speak to a sparrow, a shark can chat with a salmon, a monkey can gossip with a caterpillar, and so on. It's one of the marvels of the animal kingdom that the news has yet to do a program about.

So it was therefore a surprise to Mr. McNumpty when there was no answer. The eyes stared at him without blinking and then disappeared. And a rather pungent aroma seemed to float closer and get up everyone's nostrils.

"Oh!" said Mr. McNumpty. "That's strange . . ."

"Let me try," said Mrs. Bold, and she cleared her throat.

"Mr. Fox? I know you're here somewhere. We don't mean to frighten you. Forgive us for calling on you uninvited, but there's something we think you ought to know. You see, we live on Fairfied Road and— ouch!" A sharp pain struck the back of Amelia's hind leg.

"Ow!" cried out Bobby, spinning around.

"Aaagh!" shrieked Betty.

"Ooh!" exclaimed Mr. Bold.

Everyone, it seemed, was being nipped on their ankles, one after the other, apart from Miranda, who was perched safely on Uncle Tony's shoulder. Mr. McNumpty was probably bitten too, but his fur was so thick he didn't notice. Everyone else was hopping about clutching their legs and wondering what on earth was going on, when an unfamiliar voice—rough and angry—hissed, "Now clear off and don't come back, or I'll bite you properly next time!"

There was a rustling of ferns behind them and the sound of whoever it was stealthily running away.

"Everyone all right?" asked a concerned Mr. McNumpty.

"Betty? Bobby? Come here, dears. Let's have a look at your legs. Teeth marks! What a horrid fox!"

As the attacker had said, they weren't "proper" bite marks—no blood had been drawn—just warning nips. But it was a shock nevertheless.

"But we were only trying to help!" cried Betty.

"To save him from the pest control people!" Bobby pointed out. The twins were both tired and upset with the way the mission to help a fellow animal had turned out.

"Foxy no nicey," said Miranda, shaking her head.

"No. Not nice at all," agreed Uncle Tony. "I will probably have a noticeable limp for several days."

"Come on, everyone," said Mrs. Bold. "Let's get home before he bites us again. We're not going to be able to warn him after all."

"Good riddance," muttered Mr. McNumpty.

It was very late when the Bolds got home after this unsuccessful trip to Bushy Park. They were all a little out of sorts, not to mention tired, so the twins were given a drink of milk and then everyone went straight to bed.

Chapter

8

The Bolds were all still feeling a little sorry
for themselves the next morning over a rather
late breakfast when Minnie came to visit with
Walter, whom she'd been taking for a walk.
I say walk, but Walter didn't like to walk more
than a few meters. He liked to be carried,
preferably tucked inside
Minnie's jacket, which
is where he was this
morning.

The twins told
Minnie about the
late-night trip

to help the foxes and the rather unpleasant welcome they'd received.

"Gosh," said Minnie. "What a bad-tempered old fox."

"But the worst of it is," said Betty, rubbing her ankle, "we didn't get to tell him about the pest control van."

"He wouldn't listen!" said Bobby. "He still doesn't know the danger he's facing."

"Oh, don't bother about him," said Snappy the goose, who had been trying for several minutes to get some marmalade out of the jar with his beak. "Foxes get all they deserve. I have no sympathy for them."

"That's not very kind," said Miss Paulina.

"Well, it's true. My grandfather was killed by a fox, and so were two of my aunts. It's about time they got a taste of their own medicine. The humans are talking sense on this. I'm glad I'm going to be a human."

Mrs. Bold raised her eyes and Mr. Bold shook his head.

"I once heard a wonderful story about a fox and a goose and the power of prayer," said Miss Paulina.

"Not now," said Craig the wild boar, who was feeling rather bad-tempered over not being invited to the park the night before.

Minnie thought for a moment. "Well, from the sound of it, there's only one thing that interests this fox."

"What's that?" asked Mrs. Bold.

"Food!" said Minnie. "Did you take along a few tasty treats?"

"No," shrugged Mrs. Bold.

"Well, look at it from the fox's point of view," said Minnie. "You crept onto his home turf in the dead of night. That frightened him for starters. He probably thought you were trying to trick him. Catch him, even. He knows foxes are not very liked around here. If you'd offered him some food he might have stayed around to listen to what you had to say."

"Good point!" said Mr. Bold. "I know he likes cheese sandwiches, so let's take him some of those! I'll start making some right away."

"The other thing is . . . How can I put it?" added Minnie, looking awkward.

"What? Out with it!" encouraged Mr. McNumpty.

"Well, foxes have a very good sense of smell, don't they?" began Minnie.

"So do we," interrupted Mrs. Bold. "We are hyenas, after all."

"Well, exactly. He'd have smelled you, you see. And Mr. McNumpty. You might all be dressed as humans, look like humans, and sound like humans, but to a fox's sensitive nose you're still a bunch of hyenas, a grizzly bear, and a marmoset monkey! That must have been rather alarming and confusing for him."

"Can't do much about that, can we?" said a slightly offended Betty, giving her armpit a suspicious sniff.

"Are you saying we're all a bit *smelly?*" said Mrs. Bold, just as indignantly.

"No, not to me," Minnie replied hastily. "But maybe to a fox you are."

Mr. Bold decided it was time for a joke.

What did the left eye say to the right eye?

Between you and me, something smells!

Everyone enjoyed this joke, so he tried another.

How many skunks does it take to make a big stink?

Quite a phew!

"I think our hyena smell is very nice," said Bobby.

"Well, I think my grizzly smell is very attractive too," said Mr. McNumpty. "But I take Minnie's point. Maybe we didn't think through our visit to the foxes properly."

"So to sum up," said Mrs. Bold, jumping in before her husband told more jokes and everyone forgot about the problem at hand,

"Dangerous as it is, we should have gone in daylight; we need to take sandwiches; and we should all have a good scrub in the bath. And I've got some perfume we can all have a generous squirt of before we go."

"What's it called?" asked Bobby suspiciously.

"Well, your father bought it for my birthday. It's called An Evening in Paris."

"Eew!" responded Bobby. "I'm not spraying myself with that!"

"Well, your mother bought me some aftershave. You can use that instead," said Mr. Bold.

"And what's that called?" Betty asked.

"An Afternoon in Hampton Wick."

"Right then, twins. That's enough talk. Upstairs to the bath, please," said Mrs. Bold.

What bird steals soap from the bath?

Robber ducks!

Several hours later, after everyone had bathed and scrubbed and perfumed themselves, and Mr. Bold had made plenty of cheese sandwiches, they set off, much like any other family going for an outing to the park. As it was a hot summer's day, Mrs. Bold wore one of her own hats—a large white umbrella-like arrangement, with garlands of flowers draped around it and several life-like pigeons perched on top.

When they got to the area where the foxes lived, they spread out the picnic blanket and placed the sandwiches and some cakes enticingly on it, then retreated a few yards to watch. They were hoping that no one saw them. They certainly didn't want to draw attention to themselves or be seen talking to a fox, so they moved as far away as possible from other people, and Miranda kept watch up in a tree.

They didn't have to wait long. Within a minute a furry snout emerged from the ferns, twitching with interest. The large, well-fed fox then glided into view and headed straight for the Bolds' sandwiches. He had a quick sniff and then began to gulp them down.

"Ah, hello there!" said Mrs. Bold cautiously. "We thought you might like a cheese sandwich. Don't mind us . . ."

The fox stared coldly at Mrs. Bold, then at Mr. Bold, Bobby and Betty, Uncle Tony and Miranda, Mr. McNumpty, and finally Minnie. Walter gave a little whimper and retreated inside Minnie's jacket.

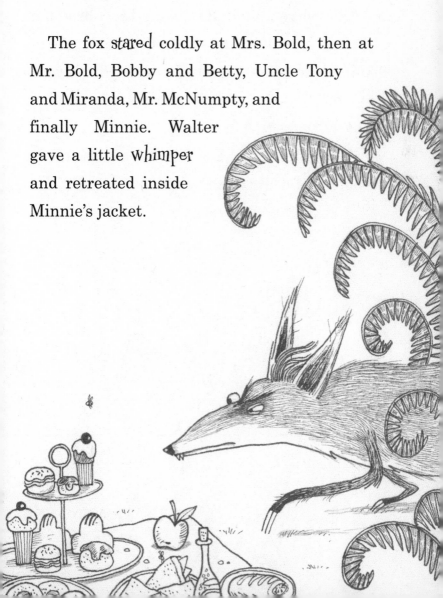

The fox's eyes narrowed and he curled his lip, revealing a row of sharp white teeth.

"Er, we're the Bolds," said Fred brightly. "From Number 41 Fairfield Road. We're animals too—well, most of us are. What's your name?"

"Mossy," grunted the fox, his mouth full of whole wheat bread and cheddar cheese. Then he looked behind him, toward the ferns, and gave a gruff call.

Another slimmer, more elegant fox obeyed his call and, although startled by the audience, nevertheless approached the picnic blanket and delicately helped herself to a sandwich.

"She's Sylvie," said Mossy, nodding his head in the direction of the female fox. "Whaddya want? Hurry up!"

"Pleased to meet you both," said Mrs. Bold. "We've come to warn you. You've upset some of the people on Fairfield Road."

"Ha!" said Mossy, unconcerned and pausing to spit out a piece of pickle that wasn't to his liking. "Good!"

But Sylvie seemed to understand, and

nodded at Mrs. Bold to continue. "Is it the stealing?" she asked quietly. "I've tried to tell Mossy." She glanced at the bigger fox, but he rolled his eyes.

"She's right, Mossy," said Mr. McNumpty. "We're animals too, and we understand the need to find food wherever you can, but you've gone too far."

"Oh really?" said Mossy, sitting back on his haunches for a moment as he contemplated a cake. "How's that?"

"Going through garbage bins is one thing. We've all done it."

"Well, I certainly haven't!" said Minnie.

"No, well, most of us have. But you've gotten too bold, Mossy. Too greedy. You've been going into people's houses, taking food from their tables!"

"Digging up vegetables!" said Uncle Tony.

"Going through cat flaps!" said Bobby.

"In broad daylight!" said Betty.

"And now the humans are going to do something about it," said Mr. Bold.

Mossy flicked a fly away from his ear and began to eat his second cake. "I'm shaking from head to paw, really I am," he said sarcastically. "Now let me guess . . . Are they going to store the food away in Tupperware boxes? Lock the cat flap? Stay up all night waiting for me with a catapult?"

"No, it's far worse than that," said Mrs. Bold.

"Oh, horror of horrors, are they sending for the pest control van? A couple of silly old fools in nylon overalls who will set a trap baited with a spoonful of cheap cat food and expect me to fall for it? Don't make me laugh!"

"I don't think you realize the danger you're in. Or the danger you're putting Sylvie in," said Mr. McNumpty gravely. "This is *serious*."

"Perhaps we should listen to them," said Sylvie, looking pleadingly at her fellow fox. "They've come here to help us. And they are the Bolds. Famous for helping animals everywhere."

"Stop whining at me, vixen!" said Mossy, wiping his snout on the picnic blanket and belching loudly. "Yes, I've heard of you Bolds. Everyone has heard of you. But do you want to know something? I think you're a disgrace to your own kind."

The Bolds all looked at each other in astonishment. Wherever they went, animals usually thanked them, admired how they had made a new life for themselves, or at the very least gave them a conspiratorial wink. They'd never had a reaction like Mossy's before.

"Why do you say that?" asked Mr. Bold.

"Just look at you all for a start: dressed up, teetering around on your hind legs, reeking of some awful perfume that I wouldn't use to freshen up my toilet. If I had one. Your relatives in Africa would wet themselves laughing if they could see what you've become," sneered Mossy. "Namby-pamby, middle-class yapping yuppies."

"Oh, I say!" said Mrs. Bold. "Really!"

"Did I ask you to come around here sticking your snout into our business? No, I didn't!" Mossy was getting worked up now. He stood, then paced menacingly toward the Bolds. Mrs. Bold pushed the twins behind her, and Mr.

McNumpty stood forward, ready to protect his friends should things turn nasty.

"I'm not going to hurt you," taunted Mossy. "I wouldn't waste my energy."

"We've just come to warn you, that's all," said Uncle Tony reasonably. "Hunt a bit more. Scavenge. Eat slugs and birds like country foxes do. Then no one will mind you being here."

"It might be healthier for us too," agreed Sylvie, glancing at Mossy's big stomach. Mossy shot her a warning glare.

"Why go to all that bother?" he sneered. "There's far tastier food for the taking on Fairfield Road. I had a nice pork chop for my breakfast, conveniently left on the kitchen counter at Number 28 with the back door wide open." He rubbed his tummy at the memory.

"And a pint of milk from the doorstep at Number 14 washed it down nicely."

"You a thief! People no likey!" said Miranda bravely, from the safety of Uncle Tony's shoulder.

Mossy leered at the monkey as if she might make a tasty snack one day.

"She's right, though," pleaded Sylvie. "We'll pay for all this stolen food one day. The humans might trap us and send us far away. Somewhere awful. Like Chatham."

"We're foxes, remember?" Mossy said to Sylvie. He shook his mane of dark red fur and looked proud and regal. "We're not pretending to be something we're not, like this lot. So *what* if people don't like us and are coming to hunt us down? That's always been the case. People don't like foxes and they never have. Nothing is going to change that. But we can outfox the lot of them. Just you see."

"But if they catch you, we think they're planning to kill you," warned Mrs. Bold.

Sylvie's eyes widened in shock.

"No surprise there," said Mossy. "Humans love killing foxes. Both my grannies were killed in fox hunts, and my uncle escaped one but was never the same afterward. Went mad, he did. We'll just have to make sure we don't get caught then, won't we?"

"Is there nothing we can say to change your mind?" asked Mrs. Bold.

"Nope," said Mossy. "Thank you for the sandwiches and the cakes. Very considerate of you. I'm almost sorry I bit your ankles last night." He laughed quietly to himself. "But not quite. Say goodbye to the Bolds and their friends," he instructed Sylvie.

Sylvie looked sadly at the visitors and shrugged. "Goodbye. And thank you for the warning. We will be extra careful from now on."

"Let's go," Mossy commanded gruffly. "Those raspberries in the forest should be ripe by now."

And with that, they disappeared silently into the ferns, just the occasional quiver in the greenery revealing their route.

Chapter

After all the unpleasantness from Mossy, everyone agreed they needed cheering up, so a visit to the swings was agreed upon.

As they walked across the park, Mr. Bold made everyone laugh with some jokes.

Why did the chicken cross the playground?

To get to the other slide!

What do you get when you cross a parrot with a centipede?

A walkie-talkie!

By the time they reached the playground, everyone was in a far better mood, and Mossy and his nasty remarks were almost forgotten.

The twins had a rather vigorous game on the seesaw, where they bounced up in the air rather alarmingly and Mrs. Bold had to tell them to calm down. Minnie and Walter went on the slide over and over again and so did Miranda, who didn't bother going up the ladder each time but leaped up the slide instead, much to the amazement of the other children and parents.

Mr. and Mrs. Bold really wanted to join in and were itching to go on the swings, but there was a big sign saying the facilities were only for children aged twelve or under. Instead they "helped" the twins on the seesaw, one on either end, catching them after they flew up in the air, and laughed and whooped as if they were children themselves.

"I wonder what will happen to those foxes," pondered Uncle Tony as he and Mr. McNumpty enjoyed an ice cream each, watching the fun from a bench.

Mr. McNumpty shook his head. "I have a rather bad feeling about it. We've tried to help them. Told them about the danger they're in. But they won't listen. I don't know what else we can do," he sighed.

"When I was a pup back in Africa," remembered Tony, "my mother told me not to eat the berries that grew on a certain bush in the rainy season. But they were big and juicy and looked delicious. I was hungry one day and decided that just one or two wouldn't do me any harm. So I ate them."

"No!" gasped Mr. McNumpty. "What happened?"

"I turned green, apparently," said Uncle Tony, shuddering at the memory. "I was sick for a week. Both ends . . ."

"I expect you listened to your mother after that?" chuckled Mr. McNumpty.

Tony nodded. "I certainly did. But I wish I'd listened to her before."

The old friends sat in silence while they contemplated what the future might hold for the two foxes. As things turned out, they were not going to have to wait long to find out.

Over the next few days there were more incidents of theft and vandalism on Fairfield Road, and the residents were outraged. POW TO PESTS couldn't come until Friday, and in that time Mossy seemed to be getting more and more daring in his raids. Something crept up on a schoolgirl one morning as she waited for the bus and raided her backpack, silently taking her lunchbox before she noticed. A man eating a kebab outside a café one evening had it snatched from his hand by what he described as "a flash of fangs and fur." And a birthday celebration barbecue was in ruins after the cooler containing all the meat and sausages was dragged into the undergrowth when the cook wasn't looking and emptied of its entire contents. They had to make do with salad and a loaf of bread, which wasn't much of a party. The local paper ran a front-page headline: **FOX FURY ON FAIRFIELD ROAD**. And Mr. and Mrs. Bingham urged Pow to come as soon as they could.

Rumor had it that Mr. Bingham was actually seen desperately urinating all around his yard one night—but I don't know for sure, and he denied ever doing such a vulgar thing, apart from in his toilet, obviously.

Finally Pow arrived on the scene and their sinister pest control vans were soon patrolling the streets of Teddington. Large metal cage traps were set in several yards on Fairfield Road and baited with pet food. Once a fox was trapped, it would be driven miles and miles away into the countryside to meet its fate.

The Bolds could do nothing but watch in horror.

"Mossy said they wouldn't fall for anything so simple, didn't he?" asked a worried Betty.

"Yes, dear. He did," said Mrs. Bold.

"I know he's not very nice, but no animal deserves to be caught like that, does it?" said Bobby.

"No, son," agreed Mr. Bold. "He might be rather rude but he's still a living creature, and I would do anything to save him."

"And what about Sylvie?" asked Betty. "She seems really nice. What if she falls for the bait and gets trapped?" She began to cry.

"There, there," said her mother. "We'll think of something. We won't let those cruel humans hurt fellow animals."

But it seemed that maybe Mossy was right and the pest control people really were nothing for him to worry about. Several days passed, and according to the gossip on Fairfield Road, not a single fox had been caught.

"Not so much as a field mouse!" huffed Zoe Bingham when she and her husband bumped into Mr. Bold on Teddington High Street. "The traps are useless and the thefts are still continuing. Why, a fox even had the nerve to pee in my yard when I had my nice clean washing hanging out."

"Are you sure it was a fox?" said Mr. Bold, giving Mr. Bingham a wink.

Mr. Bingham blushed. "I think we're going to try some different bait tonight," he said, changing the subject. "I hear this fox likes cheese."

"Oh no, foxes hate cheese," said Mr. Bold hurriedly. "Never touch the stuff."

"That's not what I heard," said Zoe through pursed lips, and she stalked off, her husband running behind to catch up.

Chapter

It seems though that the change in bait had an effect because that very night something happened. It was a wet, thundery night and everyone was fast asleep in the Bolds' household when a frantic scratching and high-pitched whining were heard at the kitchen window. Miranda, the marmoset monkey, noticed it first. She was a light sleeper anyway, and that night she had curled up on the stairs to sleep. She crept into the kitchen and saw paws banging on the glass and heard urgent, pitiful crying. She quickly leaped up the stairs and onto Mr. and Mrs. Bold's bed, where she prodded them both awake.

"Scratchy knocky knocky in kitchen! You come quick!" she cried in her high-pitched monkey voice. "Someone in trouble!"

"Oh dear, Miranda!" said Mrs. Bold, reaching for her dressing gown. "It's the middle of the night!"

"I'll go first," said Mr. Bold gallantly. "That reminds me . . ."

What woke the ghost up
in the middle of
the night?

Coffin!

Miranda chortled but Mrs. Bold said,
"Not now, Fred, please!" as she picked up
the flashlight.

Down in the kitchen the scratching was
even more frantic, the paws just a blur through
the glass.

"What is it?" asked Mrs. Bold, shining the
beam of the flashlight toward the source of
the noise.

"Me scaredy!" said Miranda, jumping on top of the fridge for safety.

"Who's there?" asked Mrs. Bold.

"Ice cream," answered Mr. Bold.

Ice cream who?

I scream every time I see a ghost!

Suddenly the scratching stopped and a pair of large desperate amber eyes peered through the kitchen window.

"Mr. Bold?" said an agitated voice.

"Quick, open the door, Fred," said Mrs. Bold. "I think it's Sylvie."

"Hold on, my dear!" called Fred, as he slid open the bolt and turned the knob. At last the door was opened and a panting Sylvie flung herself on the doormat. She was covered in mud and soaked to the skin, and there were several bloody gashes on her face.

"Oh, poor Sylvie!" said Mrs. Bold. "Come inside quickly. Whatever have you done to yourself?" She reached for a kitchen towel and began to gently wipe the mud from Sylvie's fur.

Just then the kitchen door swung open again, and there was Mr. McNumpty from next door, dressed in striped pajamas and a tartan dressing gown with matching nightcap.

"What's all the commotion?" he asked.

"It's Sylvie," said Mrs. Bold. "Something has happened."

"You've got to help me," said the fox. "Mossy's been caught in a cage trap."

"Oh nooo! Foxy twappy!" wailed Miranda.

"This is very bad news," said Mr. McNumpty.

"Don't worry, Sylvie. We'll help," said Mr. Bold, patting the bedraggled fox on the shoulder. "Where is he?"

"In the backyard at Number 10. I've been trying to chew my way through the wire, but it's no good. And Mossy . . . He's raging. Screeching and . . ." She couldn't go on.

"Don't worry. We'll go there and unlock the door. He'll be free in no time," said Fred. But Sylvie shook her head.

"It's not that simple. Those humans who live at Number 10—"

"Richard and Zoe?" offered Mr. McNumpty. "Dreadful couple."

"Whatever their names are. They've been watching through the window. They're thrilled to see a fox caught in their evil trap. Jumping up and down with delight, they are. How can we get Mossy out with *them* watching?"

"But it's three o'clock in the morning!" said Mrs. Bold. "No one will see us."

"They'll be on guard until the pest control people come to take him away in the morning, for sure. I heard them say as much. The man said he was going to make some strong coffee so that they stay awake."

"Well, we could follow the van in our little Honda, watch where they take Mossy in the countryside, and rescue him," offered Mr. Bold.

"We might lose him on the way," Amelia pointed out. "And arrive too late."

"Please hurry," said Sylvie, her voice

cracking with emotion. "There must be something we can do."

There was a thoughtful silence.

"I have an idea!" said Mr. McNumpty suddenly.

"Really?" said Sylvie, a glimmer of hope in her eyes.

"Yes. It's a long shot, but it just might work. Miranda? You go and wake everyone up. And I mean everyone. The students too. For this we're going to need all hands on deck."

"What is the plan?" asked Mr. Bold.

"I'll tell you in a minute. Meanwhile, you and Mrs. Bold must take your clothes off."

"Nigel!" said Mrs. Bold, aghast.

"Just do as I ask, please," said Mr. McNumpty firmly. "If this is going to work, everyone must follow my instructions exactly."

By then a bleary-eyed Uncle Tony, Bobby, Betty, Craig, Miss Paulina, and Snappy had gathered in the kitchen, yawning.

"Listen up, everyone," said Mr. McNumpty, sounding like a stern sergeant major in charge of his fearless troops. "It's now half past three in the morning. We don't have much time. Here's my plan . . ."

Can you guess what Mr. McNumpty's plan was? I'll give you a clue. What are Richard and Zoe most afraid of? Foxes? But more than that—WILDLIFE! Anything that might disturb their neat suburban lifestyle. So what might distract them from guarding Mossy long enough for the Bolds to rescue him? Yes. LOTS AND LOTS OF WILDLIFE! I think I've said enough, don't you? I don't want to spoil the excitement of what's to come. And come it will. On the next few pages . . .

Sylvie was too traumatized to contribute to the rescue plan, Mr. McNumpty decided, and he told Uncle Tony that it was his job to remain at Number 41 to look after her.

"Some sweet milky tea might be in order," he instructed his friend.

"As for the rest of you, this is Operation Free Mossy. Mossy is currently trapped in a cage in the backyard of Number 10. Mr. and Mrs. Bingham are situated at the rear of the property, drinking coffee by the French windows. Our strategy is to distract them and give them reason to move from this vantage point so we can liberate Mossy.

"I envision a three-pronged attack. Snappy, Craig, and Miss Paulina, you are first in— Bait and Distraction. Mr. and Mrs. Bold, you are Espionage and Counterattack. Bobby and Betty, you are Raid and Seize. When I give the command, you approach the cage, release the door, and guide Mossy to the safety of the kitchen at Number 41. Then the operation will be complete. Are there any questions?"

It was all getting a little serious for Mr. Bold, and I'm afraid he couldn't resist.

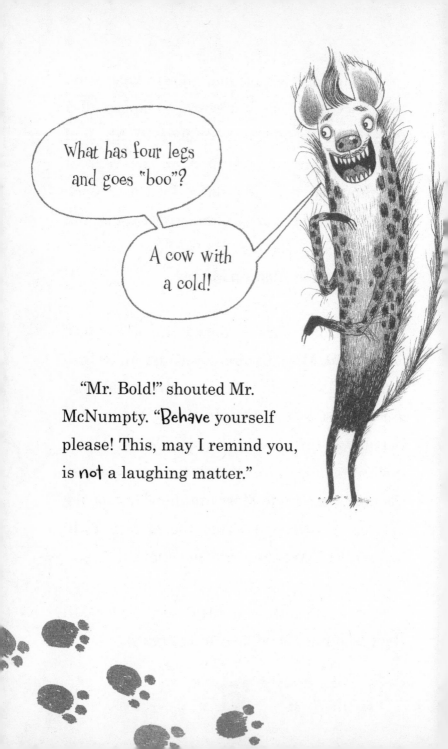

What has four legs and goes "boo"?

A cow with a cold!

"Mr. Bold!" shouted Mr. McNumpty. "Behave yourself please! This, may I remind you, is not a laughing matter."

Chapter

So here is what happened.

Richard and Zoe Bingham were sitting
in their pajamas by the French windows at
Number 10 enjoying a pot of coffee and some
cookies while keeping an eye on Mossy in the
cage trap to make sure he didn't escape. They
had waited so long for something to be done
about the foxes, they were too excited to sleep
anyway, and they were both secretly thrilled
that it had been in their yard that one was
finally caught. Richard had gone outside
briefly (wearing his boots and a plastic hat) to
poke through the bars of the cage with a stick,

but Mossy had bared his teeth before grabbing hold of the stick and snapping it in two. "A savage beast and no mistake," concluded Mr. Bingham before returning to the safety of his living room.

Zoe had just poured a second cup of coffee and asked Richard if he would like a chocolate donut when, to their astonishment, a large white goose waddled into view and began to honk loudly.

"Good heavens!" said Mrs. Bingham. "There's a goose on the patio!"

"Lord above, so there is," exclaimed her husband.

Following Mr. McNumpty's instructions, Snappy then waddled right up to the glass and began to peck, all the while honking and quacking angrily.

"He's trying to break in! Shoo!" said Mrs. Bingham, putting down her coffee cup. "Do something, Richard!"

Richard banged on the glass from his side. "Go away, you noisy bird!" he shouted, but this just seemed to make Snappy even more agitated. Snappy banged and pecked on the glass with increased speed and started to flap his wings to add to the sense of chaos.

While the Binghams were distracted, Miss Paulina was scurrying around the side of the house looking high and low for what Mr. McNumpty had told her to find. "Oh dear," she muttered to herself. "This does seem a rather naughty thing to be doing. But if it is for the greater good, then I must." Finally she found what she was looking for: the telephone wire. With her sharp otter teeth she chomped through it in a single bite. Having completed her mission, she followed the next part of her instructions and gave a loud whistle.

At the back of Number 10, Mrs. Bingham was getting quite upset. "He's scratching the glass!" she said. "Why is he doing this? Where did he come from? It's the middle of the night!"

Mr. Bingham didn't know what to do about the angry goose that was attacking his property. He tried shouting, "Boo! Boo! Go away!" He jumped up and down, mimicking the goose and barking. But with no success.

Then suddenly, on hearing the whistle from Miss Paulina, Snappy stopped snapping. He did a big, wet goosey poop for good measure, then hurtled around the side of the house to the front door. So far everything was going according to plan. But his work wasn't done yet. Now he jumped onto the front doorstep and began to pound on the front door with his beak.

This was the signal for Craig, who had been hiding behind the hedge of Number 12. He no longer wore the pink slim-fit shirt or the inside-out pants. He was on all fours and looked every inch the wild boar he really was. He strolled into the middle of the Binghams' front yard and began to dig up the flower bed with his hooves.

Alerted by the banging on the front door, Mr. and Mrs. Bingham had left their living room and rushed fearfully to the bay window at the front of their property. Too scared to open their front door, they pulled back the fancy net curtains, peering around at their porch to see what on earth was happening now. But the first thing they saw was Craig, his muscular, hairy, gray back glistening in the rain, his big porky mouth full of marigolds, stomping on what was left of their summer flower display.

"W-w-what is THAT?" said Richard. "Something wild and prehistoric!"

Zoe opened her mouth to scream in horror, but no sound came out. Disappointed by the reaction and fearing that he maybe hadn't been noticed, Craig moved to the perfectly manicured lawn and began to gouge the velvety green surface with his tusks.

"Nooo!" pleaded Mr. Bingham. "Not my lawn too! What on earth is happening?"

"We're being invaded," croaked Zoe. "Call the police, Richard. Tell them we need an armed officer here right away! And hurry! I don't think I can take much more. My knees are beginning to buckle . . ."

Mr. McNumpty had been watching the operation, hidden between some parked cars on the other side of Fairfield Road with the remainder of his troops.

"Right," he whispered urgently. "So far, so good. Bobby and Betty, you're next. Action!"

The twins darted across the deserted road and hid themselves in the shadows at the side of the Binghams' garage.

"Ready, sis?" asked Bobby breathlessly.

"Ready!" said Betty. They both hunched down in preparation, counted "One, two, three!" in unison, and leaped onto the garage roof. Then, tummies pressed to the tiles, they crept catlike to the far end and slid down into the cover of a hydrangea bush.

"There he is!" breathed Betty, pointing to the far end of the Binghams' backyard. "By the compost heap!"

"I see him. Poor Mossy!" said Bobby. The fox,

with nowhere to hide from the torrential rain, was sitting in a puddle, bedraggled and shivering. There looked to be very little fight left in him.

"Won't be long, Mossy!" said Betty in a loud whisper. "We're coming to get you out of there." Bobby went to run toward the fox, but Betty held him back.

"Wait," she cautioned. "We have to make sure the Binghams haven't come back to the living room, remember?" The two young hyenas then poked their heads cautiously out of the bush and peered toward the back of the house.

"All clear," said Betty, and they scampered across the yard toward the cage.

While all this was going on, inside the house Richard Bingham had discovered his phone wasn't working.

"The line's dead, Zoe," he said in terror.

"I told you we should have gotten a cell phone, Richard," said his wife angrily. "We've got to get out of here!" Outside they could hear the honking of a goose and the grunting of a wild boar. "This is madness. You'll have to go out there and tackle that beast yourself."

"But I can't go out THERE!" shuddered Mr. Bingham.

"Come on, Richard, for goodness' sake," said Mrs. Bingham. "Think of the marigolds."

Mr. Bingham clenched his jaw. "Very well, Zoe. If that's what you want, I will." He glanced around the hallway for a suitable weapon.

From his hideout on the street, Mr. McNumpty saw the front door of Number 10 slowly open.

A red tartan umbrella
(rolled up) poked out,
moving in circular
movements, followed
by Mr. Bingham's
dressing-gown-clad arm.

"Gerroutahere!" he shouted
bravely as his slippered feet
stepped onto the doorstep.

Craig, who was by now enjoying a luxurious
mudbath in the flower bed, raised his head
and snorted derisively.

"Go, Fred! Go, Amelia!" said Mr. McNumpty.

At his command, Mr. and Mrs. Bold—unclothed
and in full hyena cry—charged menacingly
toward Mr. Bingham, their teeth bared, jaws
drooling, piercing eyes fixed on their prey.

141

"Waaah!" screamed Mr. Bingham, and he swiftly retreated inside his front door. There was the sound of bolts being drawn and locks being turned.

By this time the twins had gotten to the cage and after a moment or two had worked out how to unlock the door.

"Come on, Mossy," they urged the hunched, broken fox. "Quickly. Come with us. You're free."

Mossy was shivering now and too cold and tired to speak, but slowly, cautiously, he got to his feet.

Mr. and Mrs. Bold, their work done at the front of Number 10, were now at the twins' side, and with their encouragement Mossy was quickly ushered through the other yards of Fairfield Road, to the back door, and into the safety of the kitchen at Number 41.

Mr. McNumpty then gave the signal to Miss Paulina, who whistled the "withdraw" command to Craig and Snappy, and Fairfield Road was quiet and empty once again.

Chapter

By now it was almost dawn, and there was a lot of cleaning up to do. The kitchen floor at Number 41 was covered in mud, and all of those involved in the rescue of Mossy were wet and cold and in need of a good bath. But no one seemed to care. Releasing their natural animal behavior had been entirely enjoyable for everyone, and the steamy, muddy troop decided that for this night only, they should just go with the flow and revel in the dirty, smelly joy of it all. Besides, getting clean and presentable wasn't their immediate priority. Mossy was.

He was set in front of the electric fire and given a bowl of water and some lamb chops. He stared into the distance while Sylvie sat by his side, but he didn't say much.

"Well done, everyone," said Mr. McNumpty, rubbing his head dry with a towel. "Top work! And in such terrible weather too!"

What happens when it rains cats and dogs?

You have to be careful not to step in a poodle!

Mrs. Bold glared at her husband.

"Mossy?" she asked. "Are you OK now?"

"I'm very mad at myself," said Mossy after a pause.

"You mustn't be," said Mrs. Bold. "Those traps are terrible things."

"Yes, but I knew that," said Mossy angrily. "How could I have been so stupid? It was the cheese. I was hungry and the smell of it just tempted me. It was Moose cheese . . . A rare delicacy. How could I resist? In my eagerness to taste it I was careless. I've stolen the bait out of those cage traps countless times before and always got away with it."

"Well, not to worry. It's a good thing we came along when we did."

"Oh, I'd have gotten out of there, don't you worry," said Mossy, not sounding in the least bit grateful.

"Mossy," said Sylvie. "That's not true. You were completely trapped in there, and if it hadn't been for these wonderful animals—"

"Oh, shut your mouth, vixen," he snapped. "They're not animals. They're wannabe humans, and I owe them nothing."

Everyone was shocked.

"Now if you don't mind, I'd like to go to sleep. I presume there's a room for me upstairs? Perhaps I can bunk in with the goose," he offered, licking his snout.

"No, no," said Snappy, suddenly not as snappy as usual. "By all means have my room," he offered. "I'll share with Craig."

"Much obliged," said Mossy. "Well, good night,

all. Sylvie, say good night."

And they went upstairs, leaving the rescuers openmouthed below.

The next day at 41 Fairfield Road there was an almighty cleanup operation. All the residents and guests had to be showered, dried, and brushed, after which the kitchen, bathroom, and more or less the whole house had to be scrubbed, mopped, and vacuumed. There were several buckets full of mud and fur and a few flower petals. Mrs. Bold had an idea that these could all be recycled into some lovely hats, so they were kept outside the back door ready for when she was in a creative mood.

Fun as it had been to be "wild" again for a few hours, it was not to be repeated. The antics of the night before had been necessary to rescue Mossy, but tails must be hidden again, clothes must be worn, and everyone had to be reminded to walk and talk like humans. And no one could suppose that Mr. and Mrs. Bingham would let the matter lie. There was (what was left of) the flower bed in their front yard, for a start. Evidence of the terror they had been subjected to was there for all to see.

Uncle Tony went for a casual stroll past Number 10 midmorning, with Miranda in her stroller, and sure enough, a police car was parked outside and a reporter and a photographer were in the front yard taking pictures of Craig's muddy hoof prints. The journalist asked Uncle Tony if he lived locally and if he'd heard "anything unusual" the night before.

"Like what?" asked Tony.

"Er, a goose? A wild boar? Couple of wild dogs with frothing mouths, a bit like hyenas?" asked the reporter hopefully.

"No. But I did see a herd of elephants. And a flying saucer," replied Tony. "Never heard such nonsense!" And then he walked away chuckling to himself.

It was generally thought among the residents of Fairfield Road that the Binghams had been the victims of youthful pranks. Some rowdy students from Kingston University had maybe dressed up in costumes as a prank. Or, it was whispered, maybe too much cheese at bedtime?

Chapter

So you might think this story is almost finished: Mossy had learned his lesson and would steal from the houses of Fairfield Road no more, and life could return to normal.

But you'd be **wrong**. You can generally work out when you're coming to the end of a book because there aren't many pages left. As you can tell, we're far from done with this tale. Barely halfway through, in fact. There's going to be what is known in literary circles as a plot development. Stand by.

Mr. and Mrs. Bold thought it wise for Mossy

and Sylvie to lay low at Number 41 for a few days while everything calmed down.

"Too much fuss on Fairfield Road!" said Mr. Bold.

Mossy grudgingly agreed. Sylvie seemed pleased to have other animals to talk to, although as the days went by she began to miss living in the park. She was a shy fox, but she got along very well with Mrs. Bold, and they often had a nice chat together while Mossy was having an afternoon nap. Bit by bit she began to tell Mrs. Bold about her life in the park—and how she had ended up with the bad-tempered Mossy.

"He wasn't always like he is now," she said apologetically. "But he's angry, you see. You'll understand why when I explain. Mossy had—well, still has—a brother. Bert. They were always very close. Inseparable. Two handsome, intelligent foxes. Strong and fit. Much admired and respected by all the other foxes. They would hunt together in the park, flirt with us vixens—me in particular. In fact Bert was my first true love. I always believed we'd end up together. But Bert was ambitious. He wanted more out of life. Like yourselves. Bert thought his best chance of doing that was as a human. He tried to persuade me and Mossy that we could live a different life, but we didn't feel the same way, and I don't think we believed he would ever do it.

"Then one day he did. He left. Mossy and I were brokenhearted. Mossy took it badly. He was grief-stricken and very angry."

"So that's why he's so rude about our way of life!" exclaimed Mrs. Bold.

"Exactly." Sylvie nodded sadly. "Mossy and I became closer in our grief. And when I realized Bert wouldn't be coming back, I agreed to be Mossy's vixen. But he's different from Bert. Maybe it's because he's so angry. I feel disloyal saying this, but he's cruel at times, unkind and cold. And particularly when it comes to humans and their way of life."

"Oh, I see."

"Mossy won't let me out of his sight. He's afraid that I'll follow Bert one day. But I'll never do that. No offense, but I don't want to be a human."

"If you don't mind me asking, why do you stay with Mossy?" said Mrs. Bold. "He does seem rather unkind."

"I've asked myself that many times, Mrs.

Bold, and when I see how happy you are with Mr. Bold, I do wish things could be different. But deep down I know Mossy is just upset, that he can change, and that if I leave him too, he'll feel even worse."

Mrs. Bold gave the vixen a sad smile. "So you never saw Bert again?"

"Just once. He came back about a year later. He was dressed in overalls, said he had a job nearby. That life was good. He begged Mossy and me to join him. But Mossy wouldn't talk about it. Accused Bert of betrayal."

"And is that when the stealing started?" asked Mrs. Bold.

"Correct," said Sylvie. "It seems to give Mossy great pleasure to invade human homes and steal food and belongings. As if this is revenge on Bert in some way."

Mrs. Bold gave Sylvie a comforting rub on her shoulder.

"Poor Mossy. And poor Sylvie. It can't be much fun living with someone who is so miserable all the time."

Sylvie shook her head. "Well, no, it isn't. But I remember the old Mossy," she said. "He's missing his brother, that's all. Maybe one day he can be happy again. Maybe we both can. I really hope so. But it's not the same without Bert. He had a loud, joyful laugh. I can't bear to think I'll never hear that sound again." Sylvie stared into the distance, lost in her memories.

"Ah yes," smiled Mrs. Bold. "Laughter is so important in life. As a hyena, I'd have to say that it is the most important thing."

Chapter

"I'm going to make a hat today!" announced Mrs. Bold the next morning, placing the buckets of dried mud and fur on the draining board. "The twins have gone around to Minnie's house, so do you fancy giving me a hand, Sylvie?"

Sylvie looked a little nervous, Mossy was asleep upstairs. In fact, since he had arrived, he spent most of his time eating, sleeping, or teasing poor Snappy.

"Come on, Sylvie," urged Mrs. Bold. "It'll be fun. Take your mind off missing the park so much."

"Oh, well, I'm not sure I'll be any good. What sort of hat?"

"A very unusual one! Now, my dear, could you run some water from the tap into that bucket full of mud? Not too much—just enough to turn it into clay again."

Sylvie—a wild fox with no training about how to act like a human— jumped up onto the kitchen counter and turned on the tap with her teeth.

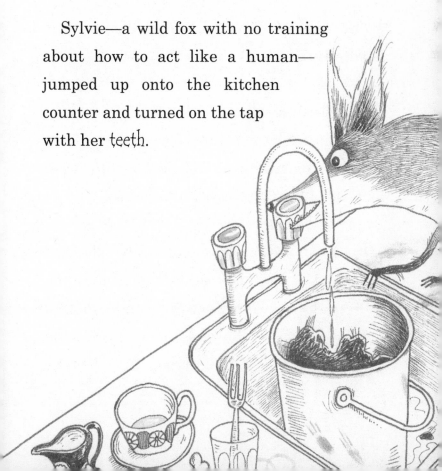

Mrs. Bold took a wooden spoon and stirred the earth with the water until it was a lovely gray, gooey mess.

"Perfect!" she announced. "Now you see that round mixing bowl? Could you pop it on your head for me please? Upside down?"

"Er, like this?" asked Sylvie, unsure. Her head was completely inside the bowl.

"Excellent! Hold still!" Mrs. Bold then got a soup ladle from the kitchen drawer and poured some mud gently over the upside-down bowl and patted it into place with her paws.

"Coming along nicely," she told Sylvie, and then got some of the fur, feathers, and squashed flowers she'd collected from Craig and Snappy and arranged them tastefully on the top. The whole creation was then gently removed from Sylvie's head and placed on a baking tray to set.

"One hat completed!" said Amelia looking admiringly at her handiwork. "And there's enough mud here for at least two more! These will go over very well with my customers at the market."

Half an hour later there were three mud bonnets sitting proudly in a row, still balanced on the draining board. Sylvie cocked her head to one side. "Pretty. But what if it rains? Won't the mud melt?"

"Um." Mrs. Bold clearly hadn't thought of this. "So glad you think they're pretty . . ." she said brightly.

Just then they heard Mossy calling for Sylvie from the spare bedroom upstairs.

"I'd better go," said Sylvie, a rather worried tone to her voice. "He's woken up. Might be hungry again."

"Can't he make his own snack?" asked Mrs. Bold innocently.

But Sylvie had jumped down onto the kitchen floor and hurried upstairs. She was back in thirty seconds. "He wants sausage and three chocolate éclairs," she said. "And he wants it now!"

Very demanding! thought Mrs. Bold to herself. *But at least he's safe here and not stealing food from anywhere.*

Mossy was certainly a hungry fox. When

Mr. Bold was trying to persuade him to stay in the safety of Number 41 for a while and not risk encountering the pest control people outside, Mossy had asked what sort of food would be provided.

"We'll feed you anything you want!" said Mr. Bold.

"Anything?" repeated Mossy suspiciously.

"Yes," pleaded Fred. "Your lives are at stake!"

"Right. Then speaking of steak, that is what I'd like. Three of them for my tea. Sirloin. Large. Organic. And then rhubarb and custard for dessert."

"Oh, er, no problem," said Mr. Bold. "I'll pop to the supermarket right away. But before I go . . ."

Did you hear about the man who went to the doctor with rhubarb sticking out of each ear and custard up his nose?

The doctor told him to eat more sensibly!

By the time Mossy had been living with the Bolds for a week, his scratches had healed and he was completely recovered. In fact, he'd eaten well and done no exercise whatsoever, so he was looking very content indeed. With no more reports of any fox thefts or invasions, the residents of Fairfield Road presumed they'd seen the last of them and life had returned to normal. The pest control vans were no longer cruising the streets of Teddington, and the sense of fear and suspicion was gone.

"I think," whispered Mrs. Bold to her husband when they were tucked in bed that evening, "it might be safe for Mossy and Sylvie to return to Bushy Park. No one seems to believe the Binghams' story of wild hyenas in the street, so hopefully everything has died down. I'll miss Sylvie, though. She's such a gentle, helpful fox and so good with the children."

"Yes, Bobby and Betty seem very fond of her too."

"I'm sure she'll make a wonderful mother herself one day, but I really think Mossy would be an awful father. He's so rude and greedy. He's a bully."

"Yes, I know. And do you know what his favorite food is?" asked Mr. Bold.

"Seconds!" chortled Amelia.

The two hyenas had to put their heads under the pillow in case their foxy visitors overheard them laughing.

"But you're right," said Fred once he was able to speak again. "So long as Mossy doesn't get up to his old tricks again, they should be fine—and it's time they left. We can't afford to keep feeding them, and Mossy is so rude about our way of life, I'm sure he'll be pleased to go. We can drop off the odd food package for them to make sure he doesn't go back to his old stealing ways, but I'm sure he's learned his lesson. He is bound to be glad to get back to the park and his life as a wild animal. We'll tell them tomorrow at breakfast. After he's eaten. He's always in a better mood then."

Chapter

15

Breakfast at the Bolds' was always a busy, jolly affair. There were three sittings, because not everyone could fit around the table at once. The twins and Mr. and Mrs. Bold were first, and they had cereal and toast with peanut butter. Mr. Bold always had some jokes to try out that he'd thought of in the shower.

> Did you hear about the man who slept under a tractor?

> He wanted to wake up oily in the morning!

Laughing with their mouths full and spluttering bits of cornflake and crumbs over the table was, I'm afraid, an inevitable side effect of such hilarity.

When the Bolds had finished, it was the turn of Uncle Tony, Miranda, and the students. Tony liked porridge with honey, Miranda enjoyed a fruit salad, and Craig the wild boar had mushrooms on toast. Miss Paulina the otter had fish, and Snappy the goose pecked at some cereal and prunes and enjoyed spitting the stones at Miss Paulina, who endured the nuisance with a saintly expression on her face. Mr. Bold usually did the dishes, but he had plenty more jokes to start everyone's day off with a laugh.

What did the cat say when he lost his money?

"I'm paw!"

What do you get if you cross a llama with a tortoise?

A turtleneck sweater!

What game should you never, ever play with unicorns?

Leapfrog!

The final sitting was for Mossy and Sylvie. Mossy didn't like to get up early, and his "order" was usually quite challenging. And that morning was no different.

"I want a fry-up today," he barked—there was never a please or thank you from Mossy. "That means jumbo sausages, three servings of bacon, two fried eggs—duck or quail, I can't abide hen's eggs—grilled tomato, button mushrooms, chocolate pudding, baked beans, and crispy hash browns. Then I'll be ready for a toasted muffin, smoked salmon with hollandaise sauce, sprinkled with chopped chives. And don't be stingy with the salmon. Then I'll finish with some crunchy granola layered with fresh strawberries, natural full-fat yogurt, and blueberry compote. And give me a freshly ground espresso while I'm waiting." Mr. Bold rolled his eyes at Mrs. Bold and started cooking.

"What about you, Sylvie?"

"Just a cup of tea please, Amelia," said the vixen, looking embarrassed. "And a slice of dry toast if you can spare it."

With such a lot of food to get through, you'd think Mossy's breakfast would take hours to eat, but once it was ready he wolfed it down hungrily and then gave a satisfied burp. Mrs. Bold nudged Fred and mouthed the words: "Do it now!"

"Ahem," began Mr. Bold. "Breakfast to your liking?" he began.

"It was OK," said Mossy. "The tomato was a little soft. And I'll have extra sausages tomorrow."

"Ah. Righto," said Fred. "Only we were thinking, once it gets dark tonight we reckon it would be perfectly safe for you and Sylvie to go home to Bushy Park. Lovely for you, eh? Get back to your old foxy ways? Bet you've missed that. Although, of course, no more stealing food from garbage bins and houses. Lesson learned, wouldn't you say?"

There was an awkward silence. Mossy stared at his empty plate and Sylvie watched him, wide-eyed with trepidation.

"I expect," continued Mrs. Bold breezily, "you must be missing your old den. Shouldn't leave it for too long. Badgers might move in. It's been lovely having you here, but—"

"GO HOME?" boomed Mossy. "You must be joking! It's not safe out there with all those dangerous humans. And I hate humans. Sylvie and I are staying put."

Mr. and Mrs. Bold's eyes widened and they stared at Mossy, then at each other. It was really a rather awkward situation.

"But having you here was only a temporary arrangement," said Mr. Bold reasonably. "We don't really have the space or money to house more animals. It can't go on forever."

"Yes, it can. And it will," said Mossy decisively. "We're *far* better off here. It's safe. We're well fed—well, most of the time. This is five-star accommodation. Maybe four and a half, given the mushy tomato. I've had to mark you down for that. Why would we want to go back to living in the park and scavenging for our dinner? We're staying here."

Mr. and Mrs. Bold did the only thing they (as hyenas) could do under the circumstances: they laughed. A forced laugh to begin with, but as the reality of the situation became apparent, with the knowledge that they were stuck with unwanted guests for the foreseeable future, a kind of desperate, hysterical laughter took hold until they were literally crying.

Mossy and Sylvie stared at them in alarm until, eventually, they pulled themselves together.

"Oh dear, do forgive us," said Mrs. Bold, wiping her eyes. "It's just that, for a moment we thought you meant you would be staying with us forever!"

"That's right, yes," said Mossy.

"You mean you'd like to become Bold students? Learn to live like humans and then, er, move on to an exciting new life?" asked Mr. Bold hopefully.

"Yuck. No. I've told you. I hate humans. I'm a fox, and I like being a fox," growled Mossy. "I'm a fox forever and this is my forever home. And that reminds me. I hate sleeping on a bed. I want a fox den in our room. Order a ton of earth, would you, from the garden center? Now I'm going to take a nap. Come on, Sylvie." Mossy then sauntered out of the kitchen. Sylvie, head bowed, followed behind him. But before Mr. or Mrs. Bold could say anything, he returned.

"And don't think about trying to get us out. We know all your secrets, remember? I'd hate to be the one who puts an end to your domestic bliss." He chuckled to himself. "Pest control would have a field day around here, wouldn't they, if your secret got out? Walking, talking hyenas and a grizzly bear! A monkey and a wild boar! You'd be on the front page of every newspaper."

"Now listen, Mossy," began Mr. Bold. "You can't be serious?"

"Shut it!" snapped Mossy. "I'm serious, all

179

right! So unless you fancy seeing your family split up and carted off to the zoo—that's if they don't shoot the lot of you—I suggest you do as I say. You've been outfoxed, mate. Who's laughing now, eh? Ha!" Mossy gave an evil laugh of his own, then cocked his leg on the kitchen door and left, his long, bushy red tail swaying from side to side as he walked regally down the hall toward the stairs.

As soon as they were alone, Mrs. Bold flung her arms around Mr. Bold, clinging to him. "Oh, Fred! What are we going to do?" she wailed. "We can't let him treat us like this!"

Mr. Bold patted his wife's back. "There now, Amelia," he comforted her. "It'll be all right. I'll think of something."

"But we can't let him blackmail us like this. It's . . . criminal!"

"I know. There must be something we can do. I need to think." Fred sat Amelia on a chair and got her a glass of water.

"And meanwhile?"

"Well, er . . ." He shrugged.

"Just don't make a joke, dear," pleaded Mrs. Bold. "I don't think there is anything that could make me laugh right now." Fred thought for a moment. But he was stumped.

"No," he answered. "For once, I don't think there is either."

Chapter

There are times when grown-ups think it best not to tell children the truth. But the children usually guess anyway.

Like if Twitchy the hamster sadly dies and the adults don't want the children to be upset, they replace it with another one that looks about the same and hope the children don't notice. Except the new Twitchy has a brown patch on his leg that wasn't there before— not to mention longer whiskers and a rather grumpy personality. So the children soon guess. They're not stupid. And sometimes the children don't want to upset their parents by telling them they've guessed there is a new Twitchy in the old Twitchy's place, and the whole thing gets rather complicated. Everyone is so busy pretending, trying not to upset everyone else, it can get rather, well, upsetting.

So while Mr. and Mrs. Bold tried to smile and carry on as normal in front of the twins, Betty and Bobby soon noticed something wasn't quite right. For a start, their parents had stopped laughing. Mrs. Bold frowned, despite herself, whenever Mossy was around, and a worried look would cross their father's face as he wrote down Mossy's latest food order. Caviar and foie gras were very expensive snacks, everyone knew that. How could their parents afford them? And why did they never say no to Mossy?

Then there was the cart full of soil that appeared on the driveway one day when the twins came home from school with Minnie.

"Is that for your garden?" asked Minnie.

"No, afraid not," said Mr. Bold, wiping the sweat from his brow as he shoveled it into a wheelbarrow. "Mossy wants it to build a den in his room upstairs."

The wheelbarrow was trundled through the house to the foot of the stairs and then Mr. Bold and Mr. McNumpty transported it upstairs by the bucketload while Mrs. Bold looked very worried about her carpet.

Mr. Bold half-heartedly made some jokes.

What did the big bucket say to the little bucket?

You look a little pail!

What's worse than raining buckets?

Hailing taxis!

The twins laughed, but Mr. McNumpty was panting for breath and didn't join in.

Moving the earth upstairs took several days.

"Why are they doing this?" Bobby asked his sister. "If I asked to build a den in my bedroom with all that muck, they'd say no for sure."

"Well, I've noticed that Mom and Dad do whatever Mossy asks," shrugged Betty.

"Me too," said Bobby. "I don't like the way he speaks to them. Or Sylvie. *Or us!*"

"He's rude and horrid," agreed Betty. "And I wish he'd move out. I know we always welcome animals to our house. And I know we're always helpful. But most animals are friendly and grateful. Sometimes I wish we'd just left him in that stupid cage."

"And he isn't making *any* effort to live like a human, so what's the point of him being here?" asked Bobby. "*And* he eats SO much food! Mom has to go shopping twice a day."

Betty nodded thoughtfully.

"There is something going on," she told her brother. "But I have no idea what it is . . ."

Then the next Saturday something odd happened. When the twins came downstairs for breakfast, Mr. Bold wasn't there.

"Where's Dad?" asked Bobby.

"Gone to work," said Mrs. Bold, pouring cereal into a bowl.

"But it's Saturday!" pointed out Betty, outraged. "We always wash the Honda together, then go to the candy store!"

"Well, not today, I'm afraid," said their mother, trying unsuccessfully to sound bright and breezy. "Overtime. There's a rush for more jokes at the Christmas cracker factory, so that'll be useful to pay all the food bills." Mrs. Bold then glanced up at the ceiling, as if the "useful" part referred to Mossy.

I'm afraid the truth was that the food bills were now so big that Mr. Bold had no option but to take on extra work at the factory, otherwise the rest of the family would have had to start going hungry.

Bobby looked despondent. He'd been looking forward to washing the car as usual with his sister and father and then choosing some chocolate at the shop.

"Never mind," said Mrs. Bold. "You can come to the market with *me* for a change and help me sell my novelty hats."

Teddington Market was held every Saturday afternoon on Church Street. It was a popular, lively, and rather trendy market: there were stalls for ceramics, meat pies, organic pet food, vintage vinyl, flowers, tasty hot food, and glittery cell phone accessories. Mrs. Bold's fancy hats stall was very popular and because her homemade hats were so unusual, people came back every week to see what her latest creations were.

Mrs. Bold, you may have heard, can make hats out of anything you might imagine: pegs, broken plates, empty baked bean tins, old clocks, dead mice: you think of it and Mrs. Bold will make a hat out of it. Smart ladies of Teddington snap up the hats each week and wear them to church on Sunday morning or to weddings or on vacation. The ladies compete with each other to see who is wearing the "latest" design, and in fashionable circles Mrs. Bold's wit and originality are much praised.

Mrs. Bold was very pleased with her latest hats, which were the mud and feather bonnets she had made with Sylvie's help following the night of Mossy's rescue. Not as tall or spectacular as some of her previous offerings, but surprisingly chic and retro in a rustic sort of way.

The twins helped their mother set up the stall and put all the hats on display.

Mrs. Bold bought the twins a hot dog each but was then rather busy with her customers. When their best friend Minnie wandered into the market, looking for a little coat for her dog Walter, Bobby and Betty were delighted.

"Hi, Betty! Hi, Bobby! Didn't expect to see you here," she said. "Don't you usually wash the car with your dad on Saturdays?"

"Dad had to go to work," said Bobby sadly. "His boss needs more jokes apparently. So we had to come and help Mom sell her hats."

"Throwing wet sponges around is definitely more fun than selling hats," concluded Betty. "We're so bored."

Minnie thought for a moment. "Why don't we help your dad?" she asked.

"How?" said Betty.

"Well, we could make up some jokes for him. And there are lots of people here at the market. Why don't we ask everyone we see if they know any funny jokes?"

"Brilliant idea!" said Bobby. "Then when Dad comes home we can tell him all the jokes we've collected!"

"And he won't need to do overtime again!" added Betty, jumping up and down with excitement.

Mrs. Bold also thought Minnie's idea was an excellent one—and it would keep the twins occupied too. There was some empty space at the end of her stall now that several hats had already been sold, so Betty, Bobby, and Minnie set up their JOKES WANTED! shop, quickly making a sign with a marker on an old cardboard box.

"Step right up! Step right up!" called Bobby. "Jokes wanted here, please! Old jokes, new jokes—we'll take them all. No joke considered too old or corny. We're not fussy!"

Betty and Minnie stood by hopefully with a pencil and notepad.

"What do we get for 'em?" asked a bald man with tattoos, who'd wandered over from the nearby fruit and veggie stall.

"Er, we'll take them off your hands for you," said Betty. "No charge!"

"They'll go to a very good home," promised Minnie. "And make people happy."

The bald man rubbed his chin. "OK," he said.

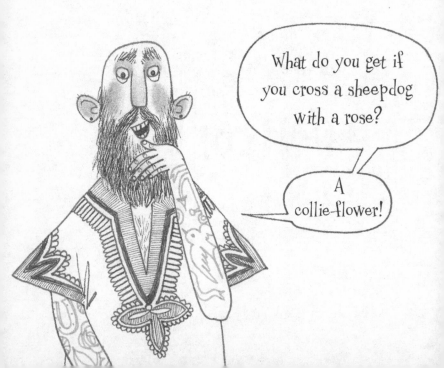

Several of Mrs. Bold's customers had overheard the joke and chuckled to themselves.

"Actually," said a woman in a floral dress, who had just purchased a turban-style hat made out of a coiled-up draft excluder with a candle stuck in the top, "I've got an old joke I'd like to get rid of." She cleared her throat.

How do you make a tissue dance?

Put a little boogey in it!

There was a roar of laughter from the bald man.

What do you call a baby monkey?

A chimp off the old block!

Soon the jokes stall had attracted a crowd and the jokes were coming thick and fast.

Why was the belt arrested?

Because he held up some trousers!

Everyone was so busy telling jokes and laughing at them, no one noticed the smart, shiny Rolls Royce that purred silently to a halt a few feet away. The tinted rear window opened a few inches and an elegant gloved hand emerged and pointed at one of Mrs. Bold's hats. The chauffeur then got out of the driver's seat, slipped through the crowd, purchased two mud bonnets from Mrs. Bold, and drove away.

Chapter

When Mr. Bold returned from work later that evening looking tired and drawn, he was thrilled with the jokes the twins and Minnie had collected for him.

"Thank you so much," he said, shaking his head in amazement. "These are great. And worth quite a lot! What wonderful pups you are."

Minnie giggled.

The twins and Minnie—who was staying for tea—felt very proud of themselves. They'd had a fun day and helped Mr. Bold at the same time. Both Mr. and Mrs. Bold looked much happier that evening.

"We'll do the jokes stall again next week, if Mom says it's OK," said Bobby.

"Yes of course, dear," said Mrs. Bold, who was making a spaghetti bolognese. "I'm all for it. And it attracted lots of new customers for my hats. I sold all three mud bonnets today and made more money than usual, which will come in handy," she said, glancing at her husband. "And it's given me an idea to make some new hats out of unusual material. How about cereal glued together with chocolate sauce? Edible hats could become all the rage."

Mr. Bold said, "Lovely. And think of all the seagulls and pigeons that will attract. Swooping down to peck at the ladies' heads!"

The thought of this made everyone laugh so much they had to have some lemonade to calm themselves down.

After tea the twins and Minnie went out to play in the yard while Mr. and Mrs. Bold cleared the table and then set it again for Uncle Tony, Miranda, and the students. Mr. Bold tried out the new jokes and everyone laughed appreciatively. Then there were more dishes to do until finally two bowls of spaghetti bolognese were placed on the floor for Mossy and Sylvie. Mossy wouldn't dream of eating from a table and wouldn't allow Sylvie to either. "We're foxes, remember?"

It was hard to forget it, these days. A pungent, foxy aroma emanated from the earth den in the bedroom and filled the whole house. You could barely open the door because of the mound of earth. There was a small round entrance

concealed behind a rose bush that Mossy had demanded be uprooted from the front yard. And because Mossy was eating so much and getting hardly any exercise, this entrance had been widened several times in the last few days.

"What's this?" asked Mossy, sniffing at his dinner suspiciously that evening. Mr. and Mrs. Bold could tell from the weary expression on Sylvie's face that Mossy was in a particularly bad mood.

"It's spaghetti bolognese," said Mr. Bold.

"Delicious!" added Mrs. Bold hopefully.

Mossy took another sniff and wrinkled his nose. "Well, I'm not eating it," he said. "Smells disgusting. Foreign muck. Make me something else."

"That's all there is," said Mrs. Bold. Mossy glared at her.

In an attempt to lighten the atmosphere, Mr. Bold asked:

Did you hear about the Italian chef who was very ill?

He pasta way!

But not even Mrs. Bold laughed at the joke.

Mossy's response was to swipe the bowl angrily with his paw, overturning it and spilling his unwanted dinner across the floor. Mrs. Bold jumped and Sylvie darted under the table for cover.

"ALL THERE IS, did you say?" growled

Mossy, his eyes flashing with anger as he moved toward Mrs. Bold. Mr. Bold jumped in front of his wife protectively.

"Now then, Mossy. No need to overreact. I'm just going to the supermarket, as it happens. What can I get you? A nice big steak?"

Mossy sat down and licked his paw.

"That's more like it," he said calmly. Then he gave a big yellow-fanged yawn. "I'll have two T-bone steaks and some crinkle-cut potatoes with sautéed carrots. Then a vanilla cheesecake. And a box of chocolates to finish."

"Of course!" said Mr. Bold. "Now why don't you go upstairs for a little nap in your cozy den, and I'll call when it's ready for you?"

Mr. Bold's obsequious manner seemed to please Mossy and a slight smile hovered on his lips. "Clean this mess up, vixen," he said to Sylvie, then sashayed out of the kitchen and back upstairs.

Being aware that any unnecessary delay might anger the hungry fox, Mr. Bold gave his worried-looking wife a hug and grabbed the car keys. "I'll be as quick as I can," he said. "Stay out of his way."

"I'll look after Amelia," said Sylvie, emerging from under the table. "You go. Hurry."

As soon as Mr. Bold had gone, Sylvie and Amelia cleaned up the spaghetti bolognese with some paper towels.

"Sorry about the mess and the waste," said Sylvie.

"It's not your fault, dear," said Mrs. Bold. But she knew the situation couldn't continue like this for much longer. Mossy was ruling the roost, and there had to be a way to fight back. They just hadn't thought of it yet.

Chapter

Mr. Bold whizzed around the supermarket, grabbing two juicy steaks, carrots, potatoes, cheesecake, and a top-of-the-line box of chocolates, and was back in the Honda in record time. He amused himself while driving home by telling himself jokes.

He was half a mile from home when disaster struck. The Honda began to cough and splutter.

"Oh dear," he said to the car. "Please don't break down now, little car. I dread to think what Mossy will do if he doesn't get his dinner!"

But it was no good—after a final shudder, the Honda's engine cut out and Mr. Bold just had time to steer it onto a side street before it stopped altogether.

Back at Fairfield Road, Sylvie and Mrs. Bold were discussing the future.

"I do feel bad about overstaying our welcome," said Sylvie. "Mossy is being very unreasonable. I've tried to speak to him about it, but he just won't listen."

"It's not your fault," said Amelia. "I know that. Everyone is welcome in our house for as long as they want to stay. It's just the cost of all the food Mossy requires and the way he treats us that is so unacceptable."

"I heard what he said to you," said Sylvie, pacing up and down and looking concerned. "He's blackmailing you, isn't he? Threatening to tell people who you really are. I'm so sorry."

Mrs. Bold nodded and a tear rolled down her cheek. "Mr. Bold says it will work itself out one day. We just have to be patient. He is not the sort to let anything get him down for long. Maybe he's right. Certainly the twins' joke stall today was a great help bringing in extra money to pay for all the, er, extras. So we'll cope, I guess. And you, Sylvie, are more than welcome here. I like having you around. And I couldn't have made those mud bonnets without you."

"Thank you. But grateful as I am for your hospitality, I'm really missing the park," said Sylvie. "The fresh air and the other foxes. Mossy must be too, underneath all the bluff and bluster. He doesn't really want to live in a human house. I will keep trying to persuade him, and I'm sure he'll decide we ought to go back soon."

"I hope so," said Mrs. Bold. "You have a right to be happy. We all do."

Mr. Bold had by now found a local garage that was willing to help with the broken-down Honda, and a man in overalls was looking under the hood. After a few minutes and a lot of tapping and some sort of twisting with a wrench, the mechanic wiped his hands with an oily rag and gave his verdict.

"Well, sir, it's your pistons. Welded against your cylinder walls, I'm afraid."

"Oh," said Mr. Bold. "Naughty pistons, eh? Will it take long to fix? Only I've got a hungry fox—I mean hungry fella at home waiting for his dinner, you see."

"I'll have to tow it back to the garage, I'm afraid," said the mechanic. "Should be ready later this week though. I'll drop you home, if it's not *too* far. Where do you live?"

"How kind of you," said Mr. Bold. "I'll tell you some jokes on the way! I live at 41 Fairfield Road. Just by Bushy Park. Do you know it?"

"Oh yes," answered the mechanic somewhat wistfully. "I know the park very well."

Mr. Bold was true to his word and the whole way back home he told endless jokes, which the mechanic thought were very funny. Jokes like:

What made the dinosaur's car stop?

A flat Tire-annosaurus!

"We're here now," said the mechanic. "I'll drop the car off in a week."

"Thank you so much," said Mr. Bold, shaking his hand and getting out of the car with his shopping. "My name is Fred Bold."

"Thanks for the jokes, friend. Brightened my day up, you have!" said the mechanic. "My name is Bert."

And Mr. Bold went indoors and cooked Mossy his two steaks, potatoes, and sautéed carrots.

Chapter

But that night Mr. Bold tossed and turned in his bed. Unable to sleep, he went downstairs for a glass of water. Mrs. Bold, realizing her husband wasn't next to her, came downstairs too and found him staring out the kitchen window.

"Couldn't you sleep, dear?" she said, putting her paw on his back.

"Oh, Amelia, this just can't go on," said Mr. Bold. "Even my children are working on Saturdays to feed this greedy animal. He's threatened *you*, he's cruel to Sylvie, and he's blackmailing us and threatening all our safety and happiness. He's a *bully*. And we're allowing him to bully us. I would **never** have let this happen in Africa. I would have stood up to a predator. But I'm so desperate to protect our way of life, I'm letting him beat me."

"I agree. But what else can we do?" said Amelia. "You're doing this to protect us. I'm quite sure if you fought it out with him you could win, my darling. But a fox and hyena fighting would alert the neighbors, and our secret would definitely be discovered. And if we throw Mossy out and demand he leave, then I'm pretty sure he'll reveal our secret without a moment's hesitation. I think all we can do is carry on as we are and hope that eventually he misses his wild ways so much he decides to move on."

"We've thought that for too long," said Mr. Bold. "We're putting up with his behavior, hoping something will change. It's what Sylvie's done for a long time, but it hasn't worked for her and it isn't working for us. We're frightened of what he will do, and we are living in fear in our own home. Well, no more."

"What are you going to do?" asked Mrs. Bold. "Please be careful. I'd rather live like this than have my family imprisoned in a zoo or a cage."

"But don't you see? We're already imprisoned—in our own home. And it's time we broke free."

"How can we stop a bully being a bully?"

Mr. Bold scratched his head for a moment.

"Well, you can't. But you can make it difficult for them. After all, there's only one of him. Together with the Bolds, Minnie, Walter, the students, Uncle Tony, Mr. McNumpty, and Miranda. That's twelve!"

"And Sylvie makes thirteen!" corrected Mrs. Bold.

"Strength in numbers! That's the answer!" exclaimed Fred, beaming at his wife. "Right. I need a pen and paper. And some cardboard and felt-tip pens . . . I'm going to be busy . . . Tomorrow things are going to be different!"

The next morning when the twins came down to the kitchen for breakfast, there was a surprise waiting for them. Hanging from all the kitchen cupboards, on the walls, and even from the ceiling were brightly colored posters. Mr. and Mrs. Bold stood huddled by the back door looking pleased with themselves, gently quivering with amusement.

It took the twins a few minutes to read the MANY posters and notices their parents had made.

"Bully-Free Zone!" said the biggest sign, above the kitchen window. As they scanned the room they read them all out loud.

"Wow," said Bobby. "This is amazing!"

"We've been rather busy," said Mr. Bold proudly. "But hopefully it will give Mossy something to think about when he comes down for breakfast."

"Er," interrupted Betty. "There's only one problem."

"What's that?" asked Mrs. Bold.

"Mossy can't read," said Betty.

There was an awkward silence.

"He can't?" said Mr. Bold.

"No, Dad," said Betty, shaking her head sadly.

"Ah," said Mr. Bold. "And Sylvie? Might she read them out to him?"

"No. Neither of them can read," said Bobby. "They're wild foxes, remember. They've never needed to learn to read."

Mr. Bold blew out his cheeks with frustration. "So, I've rather wasted my time then," he said.

"Not really," said Mrs. Bold brightly. "The twins enjoyed your posters, and I'm sure Mr. McNumpty and everyone else will too. Just, er, not Mossy."

"Yes, but Mossy is the bully in this house. That was the whole point. To try and educate him," said Mr. Bold despondently. And he began to pull down the posters and signs. Mrs. Bold and the twins helped him and then they all had breakfast together.

Suddenly Mrs. Bold cried out, "I've got it!"

"Got what?" asked Mr. Bold, somewhat alarmed.

"I've got the answer," said Mrs. Bold excitedly, throwing her toast down on the plate.

"Remember that meeting we had at the Binghams'? When everyone was talking about how to get rid of foxes? Well, someone said foxes hate lion poop, remember?"

"Yes, that's right," replied Fred. "But how does that help? We don't know any lions."

"Ah," said Amelia, raising her paw. "But we know a lion's cousin. A cougar. Remember?"

"Oh yes, Bertha, our cougar friend who runs the tea rooms down in Cornwall."

"Precisely. Well, maybe whatever it is about lion poop that foxes can't stand must surely apply to cougar poop as well. I'm sure Bertha wouldn't mind helping us."

So Mrs. Bold dialed a number and waited a moment.

"Ah, Bertha! It's Amelia Bold. I trust you're keeping well? I wonder if you might be able to help us out. A rather delicate matter . . . I'm after your poop."

And so, the next day a package arrived for Mrs. Bold, labeled "Handle With Care." Inside was a Tupperware container, and inside the container was a generous donation of

Bertha's number twos.

> Dear Amelia,
>
> Hope this does the trick and you're soon rid of that pesky fox! Love to all, your friend,
>
> Bertha.

"Bless her!" said Mrs. Bold.

"That's what friends are for!" commented Mr. Bold.

"So how is it going to work?" asked Betty.

"We'll wait until Mossy is asleep in his den, then just chuck the poop in, I suppose. And we'll leave the front door open. With any luck

Mossy will shoot out of the den in horror, down the stairs and out. Gone forever!"

"And good riddance!" muttered Uncle Tony.

"But what about Sylvie?" asked Bobby.

"Sylvie no like poo poo," pointed out Miranda. "Sylvie run away too. Big shame!"

"Well," said Mrs. Bold, "after breakfast I'll ask Sylvie to help me with some new hats. Mossy will have gone back to bed as he always does. We'll wait ten minutes, then we strike."

"Excellent plan of action," said Mr. McNumpty, who had been listening intently. "Top notch. Thought of everything."

"Right," said Mr. Bold. "Tomorrow is the day!"

Chapter

20

In the morning everyone had breakfast as usual—the Bolds first, then Uncle Tony, Mr. McNumpty, and Miranda, then the students. They all tried to act as normally as possible, but there was an air of excitement, as everyone hoped they would soon be rid of the troublesome Mossy.

Finally Mossy and Sylvie arrived. As usual Sylvie ate hardly anything, but Mossy was particularly hungry.

"Get me some chorizo tacos and hash browns and three fried eggs. Then I'll have cheddar cheese frittatas, cherry tomatoes, and thick sliced ham, and some cinnamon buns."

"Certainly, Mossy," said Mr. Bold obligingly. "It will just be a minute!"

After he'd eaten his way through the mountain of food and demanded more buns and a full-fat yogurt, Mossy belched loudly and yawned.

"Going to go and sleep it off now?" asked Mrs. Bold brightly.

"Yup," said Mossy. "C'mon, Sylv."

"Ah, Sylvie, would you mind helping me for half an hour? I'm making some new hats out of rice pudding and wondered if you'd mind doing some stirring for me?"

"Certainly, Amelia," said the vixen. "Happy to help."

"Laterz," muttered Mossy, giving his tummy a rub. Then he left the kitchen without so much as a thank you and went back to his den.

"Listen, Sylvie," whispered Mrs. Bold. "We're going to try something that will free us, and you, of Mossy."

"Whatever do you mean?" asked the startled vixen.

"Mossy has to go. He's making everyone unhappy and he's a bully. But I want you to know that you're welcome to stay with us, if you want to."

"What are you going to do?"

"There's no time to explain now, but you do understand why we're doing this, don't you?"

"I-I think so," said Sylvie.

"I'm going up!" said Mr. Bold, wearing some bright orange rubber gloves and holding the Tupperware box at the ready. Then he added: "Knock, knock!"

"Who's there?" asked Mrs. Bold.

Europe!

Europe who?

Well, that's not very nice!

Mr. and Mrs. Bold had a nervous laugh at his joke, then Fred pulled himself together. "Right. You two, stay in here. Wish me luck!"

After opening the front door wide, Mr. Bold crept up the stairs. He paused on the landing and listened to the loud snoring coming from inside the fox den, then opened the Tupperware box. He sniffed at the contents then wrinkled his snout. "Disgusting!" he thought to himself, then silently counted "One, two, three . . . !" and threw the contents deep into the den in the direction of the snoring fox, and pressed himself against the wall, ready to watch Mossy's swift exit.

The snoring stopped but nothing happened.

After a tense moment of waiting, Mr. Bold looked into the den.

"Strange, I thought he'd be out by now," he muttered, then peered in a little closer. Suddenly a large lump of cougar dung hit him splat on the nose.

"Ugh!" cried Mr. Bold. "That wasn't supposed to happen."

"Trying to scare me away with THAT?" said Mossy's voice. "You stupid hyena." And another lump of cougar poo hit Fred, who quickly retreated to the kitchen.

"It didn't work, then?" concluded Mrs. Bold, as she wiped her husband's hairy face with a dishcloth.

"Not at all," said Fred. "Mossy is still up there, settling back down for his nap. I just got covered in the stuff for my trouble."

"What was it?" asked Sylvie, her nose twitching.

"Cougar poop. I thought foxes hated the smell and that Mossy would run in terror from our house and we'd be free."

Sylvie shook her head. "Lion poop, yes. Terrifies us. Cougar poop, no. Doesn't bother us in the slightest."

"Ah!" said Mrs. Bold. Then she began to laugh. "It is quite funny though. My Fred covered in poop!"

So of course Fred laughed too. Eventually even Sylvie couldn't resist. And after a good laugh, they all felt much better. But the problem of Mossy remained and the Bolds were out of ideas.

Chapter

The next morning was bright and sunny and there was nothing to indicate that it was going to be a day of great upset and tragedy.

After breakfast Minnie came to visit the twins with her little dog, Walter, and the four of them went to play in the yard.

Mr. and Mrs. Bold were in the living room giving the students a lesson on hind-leg walking and general behavior. All three had now mastered dressing up in human clothes and talking—more or less.

Craig liked to disguise his ears under a bowler hat and was rather keen on saying "How dooo yooo dooo?" to everybody.

Walking and manners were proving to be a bit more of a challenge. But, as Mr. Bold pointed out, if Uncle Tony had managed to do it, then anyone could. The Bolds thought it would probably soon be time to let them out into the real world and see how they fared.

Mr. McNumpty and Uncle Tony were playing dominoes on the kitchen table.

Mossy and Sylvie had retired to their den after breakfast and, as usual, weren't expected to be seen again until lunchtime.

Miranda the marmoset monkey was dozing on the windowsill in the bathroom and it was she who spotted the newly repaired Honda pulling up outside 41 Fairfield Road. She had heard about the breakdown, so when she saw the man in his overalls coming up the walk, she scampered downstairs to alert Mr. Bold.

"Man come! Honda better!" she squeaked, just as the doorbell rang.

"Ah, thank you, Miranda," said Mr. Bold. Turning to the students, he said, "I suggest you all practice walking about some more. Try not to waddle too much, Snappy. It makes you look like a goose, which of course you are, but the idea is to disguise the fact. And Craig— less snorting. Miss Paulina, you're doing very well, but young ladies don't usually twitch their whiskers quite as much as you do."

"Why don't you invite the mechanic in?" suggested Mrs. Bold. "He sounds very nice, and it will be a good test for the students. A brief encounter with someone from the outside world."

"What? Bring him into the living room?" asked Fred.

"Yes, why not? Everyone ready to meet a proper human?" she asked the class. There was an excited giggle and much nodding from Miss Paulina.

"Yup!" quacked Snappy.

"If it is your wish," said Miss Paulina.

"Bring it on!" said Craig.

"Jolly good," said Mr. Bold, uncertainly. "Back in a moment!"

"I'm not sure they're ready," said a worried Mr. Bold to his wife once they were out of earshot. "But I guess there's only one way to find out . . ."

The doorbell rang again.

"Hurry up!" said Mrs. Bold.

"Coming!" called Fred, and seconds later he opened the door to the mechanic.

"Ah, Bert!" said Mr. Bold cheerily. "Do come in."

"Car all fixed up for you, bud," said Bert, stepping into the hallway. "Here's your bill. I've taken ten percent off for all the laughs you gave me." He glanced up the stairs and seemed to be sniffing the air for some reason.

"That is so kind of you," replied Mr. Bold. "Which reminds me . . ."

What did the duck say after he went shopping?

Put it on my bill!

"Ha ha ha!" laughed Bert appreciatively.

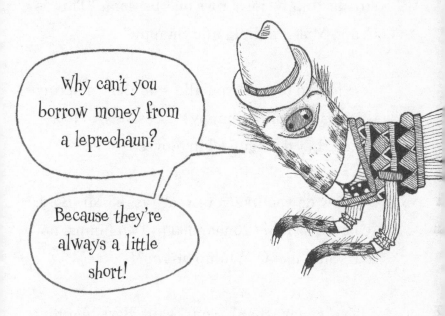

Why can't you borrow money from a leprechaun?

Because they're always a little short!

Bert laughed loudly again. Very loudly. "Oh, you're funny, Mr. Bold, you really are."

"Would you like a cup of tea while you're here?" asked Fred. "Come and wait in the living room while I put the kettle on." Mr. Bold led the mechanic into the living room and introduced him to Mrs. Bold. "My lovely wife. And we have some visitors." He indicated the three students sitting primly in a row on the sofa. "This is Craig, Miss Paulina, and Snappy."

"Pleased to meet you all," said Bert, shaking their paws—or in Snappy's case, webbed foot— which they'd disguised in gloves.

"How do you like your tea?" asked Mr. Bold. "One leg or four? I mean lump. Two lumps, not four. Silly me. One lump or two?"

"No sugar, thank you," said Bert, smiling broadly and taking a seat by the window. Mr. Bold went to make the tea and Mrs. Bold nodded at the students, encouraging them to practice their conversational skills.

"Nice day for a swim. I mean walk," said Snappy.

"Er, yes, I suppose so," said Bert.

"It's otter than you think," said Miss Paulina, who immediately realized her mistake. "Hotter, even. Forgive me. Why on earth did I mention an otter?!"

Mrs. Bold winced. This was not going well.

"Mmmm. Quite warm out," said Bert.

"You fix cars for a living?" asked Craig. "Interesting? Or boar-ing?"

Bert began to giggle. "I'm sorry," he said. "But, you see . . . Oh my . . . it's just that . . ." But his giggles got the better of him and in a few seconds he was quite helpless, throwing his head back and roaring and bellowing with laughter.

In the kitchen Mr. Bold was stirring the tea in the pot when he heard the happy sound of laughter from the living room.

"They're doing well, then," observed Mr. McNumpty, looking up from his dominoes.

"Sounds like it!" said Uncle Tony.

"He's a very nice chap," said Mr. Bold. "Liked all my jokes and enjoys a good laugh."

"Clearly!" said Mr. McNumpty. Now they could hear everyone joining in the laughter, which seemed to be getting more and more raucous.

"Whatever the joke, it sounds like a cracker!" said Mr. Bold. "I think I'd better go and write it down."

Just then Sylvie appeared in the kitchen, wide-eyed and alarmed.

"Mr. Bold?" she said urgently. "Who is that laughing in the living room?"

"Sorry if we disturbed you," said Mr. Bold. "I'll go and ask them to keep the noise down."

"No, it's not that." Sylvie shook her head. "I recognize that laugh . . ."

"Oh, I doubt it, Sylvie. You don't know him. It's just Bert who fixed the car for me."

This news seemed to make Sylvie feel faint, and she sat down on the kitchen floor. "Bert? Car mechanic?" she whispered. "Then it *is*. It's him. It's Mossy's brother, Bert."

Chapter

Mr. McNumpty's jaw dropped open with surprise.

"You mean . . . Bert is a fox?"

"I knew there was something about him," said Mr. Bold. "I just couldn't quite put my paw on it. And I was so concerned about getting back to cook for Mossy, I didn't really give it much thought."

"Well, well, well!" Uncle Tony shook his head. "He's done all right for himself, then."

"Please," interrupted Sylvie, still rather dizzy with shock. "I must speak to him. Would you ask him to meet me in the yard for a private word?" she said, and she staggered out the back door.

Forgetting all about the promised tea, Mr. Bold hurried back to the living room. The sight that greeted him was not one of civilized strangers making small talk. Far from it. Everyone was on all fours on the living room carpet, sniffing bums, rubbing snouts and beaks, and behaving very much like animals.

"Oh!" said Mr. Bold.

"Bert is a fox!" said Miss Paulina.

"He saw through our disguises almost at once," laughed Craig.

"He gets a bit tired of being a polite human all the time," said Mrs. Bold. "He couldn't wait to get down on all fours again!"

"Oh, Mr. Bold!" laughed Bert. "I knew this was a house full of animals the moment I stepped through your front door." Bert tapped the side of his nose. "Animal sense of smell, you see! And there was one animal I could smell above all the others. Fox!" He looked intently at Mr. Bold. "And am I right in thinking a certain vixen in particular . . ."

"Sylvie is waiting for you outside," said

Mr. Bold. He could tell from the excitement in Bert's eyes that this was to be a reunion he had longed for. "Come this way." Despite all his time living as a human and working as a car mechanic, Bert had immediately reverted to his natural fox-like behavior, and although he was still wearing his overalls, he trotted on four feet out of the living room and raced sleekly down the hall, through the kitchen, and out the door into the backyard.

Outside, the twins and Minnie were playing catch. They were so engrossed they hadn't noticed when Sylvie slipped out the back door and sat expectantly under a large, flowering pink peony.

The leaves of the plant trembled slightly, conveying the nervousness of the vixen concealed beneath.

But when Bert stood on the back doorstep, panting slightly, Bobby noticed him at once and wondered why there was a fox dressed in overalls in their house. It couldn't be Mossy. He was too thin.

The fox's snout twitched and he immediately turned to face the peonies. Suddenly Sylvie emerged and the two foxes came face to face on the lawn.

"It can't be!" said Sylvie.

"It is!" answered Bert.

"I thought I'd never see you again," said Sylvie. "That you were off living your new life." The vixen had tears of joy in her eyes. "How are you?"

"I'm . . . I'm fine . . . I've missed you."

The two foxes stood inches apart, their wet noses twitching with excitement and glistening in the evening sunshine.

"I didn't expect . . . What are you doing here?" asked Bert.

"The Bolds took us in after Mossy was caught in a trap. We were only supposed to stay for a little while, but Mossy likes being waited on by Mr. and Mrs. Bold."

"Mossy!" gasped Bert. "My brother! Is he here? Can I see him?"

Sylvie glanced behind Bert and looked suddenly worried. "I don't think that's a good idea. He's changed, Bert. He's been so angry since you left. He won't—" she stopped suddenly. "He's just come out. Behind you."

Bert tore his eyes away from Sylvie and turned around. There, on the kitchen step, was Mossy.

"Mossy!" cried Bert, bounding up to his brother, tail wagging beneath his overalls. "It's me! Bert! Hardly recognized you. Gosh, you've put on a few pounds since I last saw you, bro!"

But Mossy's tail didn't wag in response. It stood upright, quivering with uncertainty, and the hackles along the ridge of his back rose up.

"You," he growled quietly. "What are you doing here?"

"I work in the garage in Hampton Wick. Came to deliver Mr. Bold's car," said Bert cheerfully. "It's all a wonderful coincidence. Fate!"

Mossy's lip curled, revealing his teeth. "Get out of here. Go back to where you came from."

"What? Aren't you pleased to see me?" asked Bert, bewildered by his brother's unfriendliness.

"Mossy, be kind! Please!" pleaded Sylvie.

But Mossy jumped off the step and stood between Sylvie and Bert. "I'll not be kind to a traitor," he said.

"I'm not a traitor!" objected Bert. "I'm your brother!"

"You're no brother of mine. You left us, remember? Think you're someone now, do you? Too good to be a fox?" Mossy was getting angrier with every word. "How dare you waltz in here and start flirting with my Sylvie. You always thought you were better than me. Well, I'll show you!" Suddenly Mossy threw himself at Bert, grabbing hold of his overalls with his teeth, pulling him to the ground.

The twins and Minnie stopped their game and ran inside to get help.

"Mossy! **Stop!**" shouted Sylvie, but the two foxes were rolling around on the lawn and over the flower bed in a flurry of fangs, fur, and torn fabric. There was nothing Sylvie could do to stop Mossy's aggression—he was out of control, it seemed. As if to illustrate the fact, Mossy howled and screeched like the wild fox he was. Bert tried to defend himself, but Mossy was snarling with rage, biting and snapping viciously. Bert was on his back now, and Mossy stood over him, wild-eyed and triumphant.

"Gotcha!" he hissed, then drew back his lips and lunged at Bert, sinking his sharp teeth into Bert's shoulder. Bert gave a screech of bitter pain and slithered out from under Mossy's paws. Hunched and howling, he squeezed himself through a gap in the fence and limped off as fast as his injuries would allow.

Mossy sat panting on the lawn, covered in mud. He turned to glare at Sylvie for a moment.

"Don't even think about going after him," he commanded. "Stay where you are! I'll go." His eyes narrowed. "And I'll finish what I started." Mossy headed toward the gap Bert had escaped from, but suddenly Mr. McNumpty was there, blocking his way.

"Enough!" said Mr. McNumpty. "Stop this awful fighting at once! He's your brother."

But Mossy's eyes were still full of fury. "Get out of my way, you old fool," he spat. "Or I'll bite you too."

"I won't warn you again!" said Nigel. "This is a happy, civilized household. You can't and won't spoil that for us. You have treated my good friends badly for too long. Not to mention Sylvie. I won't stand by and watch it anymore, and I will certainly not tolerate fighting."

"Let me through the fence, or else!" barked Mossy. "I'm a wild fox and I fight and bite, so there. I hate you and the Bolds and everyone in this house of fake humans." Mossy was staring at Mr. McNumpty's leg, obviously about to bite.

Mr. McNumpty knew there was only one thing he could do under the circumstances. He raised himself up to his full grizzly bear height, puffed out his chest, and raised his front paws. His jaws opened wider than ever before and a deafening, terrifying roar shook the ground and seemed to go on forever. Mossy shrank backward, tail between his legs, eyes

squinting with sudden fear. When he was a few feet away from the suddenly terrifying Mr. McNumpty, he turned and ran, bounding down the side of the house and away.

Chapter

The whole, awful altercation had lasted less than a minute, and when Mr. McNumpty's roar finally finished there was suddenly silence.

Peering out the back door to check if it was safe, Mr. and Mrs. Bold came into the yard with the frightened twins and Minnie behind them. Walter was not only hidden inside her jacket but buried deep inside the sleeve, quivering.

"It's all right, he's gone," said Mr. McNumpty, tucking his shirt back into his trousers and straightening his tie. "Sorry about that. But it was necessary under the circumstances."

"This is all so awful," said Sylvie. "Bert ran that way, and Mossy went after him. Mossy is in such a state, who knows what he might do. I never thought he could stoop that low. What if he comes back for me?"

"I doubt Mossy will show his face here again," said Mr. McNumpty. "Not after all the trouble he's caused."

"And not after you roared at him," pointed out Uncle Tony.

"I hope not," said Sylvie quietly. "He's gone too far this time."

"We wanted him to leave, but not like this," said Mrs. Bold.

"And poor Bert is injured. He might need help!" cried Sylvie. "What will happen if Mossy finds him?"

"Fred, you had better jump in the Honda and go looking for both of them," suggested Mrs. Bold.

"Yes, good idea. Sylvie, you come with me. You'll be able to spot likely hiding places for a fox. And Mr. McNumpty too, if you wouldn't mind. In case we need a bit of grizzly bear muscle again. There's no telling what we'll find. Amelia, you stay here with everyone else. We may be gone a while."

So for the next few hours the Honda slowly cruised the streets of Teddington with Mr. Bold at the wheel and Mr. McNumpty and Sylvie glued to the windows looking intently for any trace of Bert or Mossy or any likely hiding place. The atmosphere was tense, so Mr. Bold thought it might be a good time to tell a few jokes.

Why was the broom late?

It over-swept!

How do you make an octopus laugh?

With ten tickles!

But there was no response from the passengers.

"Tough crowd," said Mr. Bold to himself. "Try this one . . ."

Why did the clock get called to the headmaster's office?

For tocking too much!

Then, as they drove along the busy Kingston bypass and had almost given up all hope of seeing either fox, Sylvie let out a sudden yelp.

"There! I saw something furry by the side of the road. Stop! Stop!"

Mr. Bold couldn't stop right at that moment, but there was a hard shoulder a few feet ahead and he pulled in there.

"You stay in the car, Sylvie. Mr. McNumpty and I will investigate," instructed Mr. Bold. But before he could open the car door, Bert, no longer in his overalls, looking disheveled, suddenly appeared at the window.

"Don't get out of the car, please!" said the distressed fox. "It's dangerous. And too awful to see. Let me in. I'll come with you and explain."

"Bert!" exclaimed Sylvie as he got in the back of the car next to her. "Are you OK?"

"Oh, Sylvie!" said Bert, gently stroking her face. "I *tried* to stop him running across the road, but he wouldn't listen. He ran straight out and a truck came and . . ."

"You mean—Mossy is . . .?"

"Yes, I'm sorry, my dear. He was struck by the truck and he died instantly."

Sylvie covered her eyes and began to wail. "Can I see him?" she sobbed.

"I think it would be better if you remembered him as he was," said Bert. "The Mossy we knew and loved in Bushy Park."

"He's right," said Mr. Bold. "Let's get you home." And he shook his head in sorrow and pulled back out into the traffic, heading for Fairfield Road.

"Why was he crossing that busy road in the first place?" asked Mr. McNumpty.

"He saw me on the other side, and he was still so angry he just wasn't thinking properly. I shouted at him to stop, but . . ."

"He always hated cars," said Sylvie through her tears. "His father was killed by one years ago. And of course they carry people around, and he always thought he was smarter than any human being. It's too awful."

There was shocked silence inside the little Honda as they drove back to Teddington. But as they reached the gates to Bushy Park, Sylvie opened the window and took several deep gulps of air, closing her eyes.

"Would you mind stopping here, Mr. Bold?" she asked politely. "I just need a moment."

It was dusk now, the sky streaked with pink. Sylvie got out of the car and wandered to the edge of the ferns, which seemed to wave as if beckoning her.

Bert followed her. "Sylvie. Are you all right?"

"There is no reason now why I can't go back to my old life in the park and live like a proper fox," she replied.

"But what about me?" asked Bert. "Could you not come and live with me in Hampton Wick? I have a lovely house . . ."

"I could if that was what I wanted. But it isn't. Living like a human is not for me, Bert," said Sylvie, looking out across the green ferns. "This is my home—here."

"But now that Mossy is gone, I thought you and I could find happiness together. My garage business is successful and, well, I love you, Sylvie," said Bert.

"And I love you too, but I'm not going to live my life doing what another fox wants me to do. I've spent too long in a life I didn't enjoy out of loyalty to Mossy. Now I need to live the life I want to lead. As a wild vixen in the park. My mind is made up," said Sylvie firmly. "I don't want the same life that you do."

Sylvie returned to the car and said goodbye to Mr. Bold and Mr. McNumpty. "Please thank Mrs. Bold for being my friend. And the twins. Everyone. I shall miss you all a great deal, but I'm not going back to Fairfield Road."

And Mr. Bold, Mr. McNumpty, and Bert watched as she wandered away into the undergrowth.

Later that night Mr. Bold and Mr. McNumpty returned to the Kingston bypass with a shovel. When no one was about, they placed Mossy's body in the wheelbarrow then drove to a quiet grassy spot on Ham Common and buried him.

Then for a few moments, the hyena and the grizzly bear stood in respectful silence over the fox's grave.

And that night the quiet of Bushy Park was disturbed by a pitiful high-pitched wail.

"But where has Sylvie gone?" asked Bobby and Betty. "Will she be OK?"

"Oh yes," their mother reassured them. "Sylvie will be fine. She just needs some time. She is free of Mossy now, though. Free to go back to being a real fox again. A fox that doesn't steal things. I know that's what she wanted."

Chapter

Several months later

All was back to normal at 41 Fairfield Road. The twins were happy and mischievous and the students were progressing well. Business at Mrs. Bold's hat stall at Teddington Market had been booming. Her "Edible Collection" was even featured in the *Teddington Gazette*. People came from miles around to see and purchase such unique headwear, and it was even suggested she might like to open a shop on Teddington High Street. Mrs. Bold was very flattered by the idea but decided she'd miss the cheery atmosphere of the market and the other friendly stallholders.

"Besides," she said. "I enjoy selling hats on Saturdays and making them on the other days. If I was in a shop every day, I'd run out of hats rather quickly!"

Then, to everyone's astonishment, a photo appeared in a posh glossy fashion magazine of two (minor) royal princesses at a horse race wearing what was unmistakably a matching pair of Mrs. Bold's mud bonnets!

The next Saturday the stall was besieged with lots of women in expensive clothes and dark glasses demanding mud bonnets. Dozens of orders were placed.

"Will we have enough mud, though?" pondered Mrs. Bold.

"We've got enough mud for a thousand hats, silly!" said Mr. Bold.

Can you guess what he was referring to? Where was there lots of dirt going unused?

So it was all hands on deck at Number 41 the following week. The twins' job was to carry bucketloads of earth downstairs from Mossy and Sylvie's abandoned den, then Mr. Bold poured in water at the kitchen sink and stirred the mud until it was just the right consistency. Uncle Tony and Mr. McNumpty

sat at the kitchen table with bowls over their heads and Mrs. Bold sloshed the mud on top, while Miranda the marmoset monkey leaped from table to counter scattering feathers on the still-wet bonnets in a tasteful, artistic manner. (Luckily, Snappy had recently molted, so there were plenty of feathers around.) Once the mud had set, the bonnets were eased off the bowls and placed on the draining board to await final touches. Dozens of mud bonnets were made ready for the next market day.

"We'll make enough money for another vacation in Cornwall!" declared Mrs. Bold.

"Hurrah!" cried the twins.

And then, as if life couldn't get more exciting, one morning Mrs. Bold received a very important-looking envelope with the crest of Buckingham Palace on it.

She opened it and gave a shriek. "We've been invited to a royal garden party!" she said breathlessly.

"Wow!" said Betty. "Whatever shall we wear?"

"Hats, of course!" said Bobby.

The big day arrived and the Bolds were beaming with pride as they lined up outside 41 Fairfield Road to get into the Honda, which had been given an especially thorough cleaning by Mr. Bold and the twins that morning.

"Before we go to the Palace, let's take a short detour through the park," said Mrs. Bold, giving her husband a knowing wink.

"The park? But we mustn't be late for the Palace," said a concerned Betty.

"There's someone we need to say hello to and thank on the way, that's all," replied Mrs. Bold. "Stop just here—now we'll all get out and wait for a moment."

"There's no one here!" said Bobby as they sat quietly in a grassy clearing.

"Hush!" said Mrs. Bold. "Be patient!"

After a few minutes there was a rustling

sound and a face peeped out through the ferns. It was a fox.

"Sylvie!" gasped Betty.

"Hello, everyone," said Sylvie. "You all look fancy. Where are you off to?"

"We're going to London, to a royal garden party. Those mud bonnets you helped me to make have become all the rage. I just wanted to say thank you and see how you're doing, after I got your note telling us you had a new den and were happy."

"Oh, it wasn't me who wrote it," replied Sylvie. "I'm a wild fox, remember?"

Sylvie moved over to where the Bolds were sitting and looked over her shoulder. Another fox followed her.

"Bert!" said Mrs. Bold. "It was *you* who wrote the note and popped it into our mailbox! Are you two . . . ?"

Bert nodded, "So glad you could pop by."

"Yes, we are a couple now," said Sylvie shyly. "Bert came to find me after . . ."

"I realized we were meant to be together," said Bert, gazing lovingly at Sylvie. "She could never live as a human, and I could never be happy without her. So I gave everything up and followed my heart. We're living here, where we are happiest, in Bushy Park. And there is something else to tell you," he added before giving a high-pitched call. A second later an adorable little fox cub scampered out of the tall grass and ran to Sylvie, its mother. Then another cub. And another. The three mischievous young cubs peered at the Bolds for a few seconds, their eyes wide with curiosity.

"It's all right," Sylvie said to them. "They're friends."

A few minutes later, protected from prying human eyes by the tall ferns, the fox cubs were climbing all over their new friends, nibbling and tugging at clothes and playing happily, tails wagging.

Everyone laughed and smiled with animal joy.

Eventually Mrs. Bold said, "We really ought to be going. The garden party, remember?"

"Must we?" asked Betty.

"This is much more fun!" said Bobby, as one of the cubs began to chew his newly made hat.

And so the Bolds never made it to the Palace. They were having their own party with the foxes.

They were having such a lovely time they didn't notice the change in the weather until heavy drops of rain began to fall.

Perhaps it is just as well they didn't go to Buckingham Palace. The sudden rainstorm took the guests at the royal garden party by surprise too. The two royal princesses, busy chatting to Lord and Lady Someone-or-other and wearing their mud bonnets, were caught in the deluge.

And what happens to a mud bonnet when it gets wet? Yes, that's right. Large brown trickles of wet mud began to drip down the royal faces.

You might think this was a disaster for Mrs. Bold and would spell the end of her hat business. But guess what? Mud is a very well-known restorative face treatment for tired skin. And the next day the princesses were positively glowing with an ethereal beauty they, quite frankly, didn't have before. And so Mrs. Bold's hats became even more popular than ever before!

So sometimes, even if things go wrong, they do, somehow, go right in the end. Funny how things work out, isn't it? And I do mean FUNNY!

The End

MR. BOLD'S JOKES

Why did the pup chase his tail?
He was trying to make ends meet!

What do you do if a pup eats a dictionary?
Take the words out of his mouth!

How do you hide a little horse?
Mascarpone!

What's huge and gray and sends people to sleep?
A hypno-potamus!

How do you tell the difference between a pup and a marine biologist?
One wags a tail, the other tags a whale!

Why was the cookie sad?
Because his mommy was a wafer so long!

How do you approach an angry Welsh cheese?
Caerphilly!

What did the cheese say to himself when he looked in the mirror?
"Halloumi!"

What did the grape say when the fox stepped on it?
Nothing. He just let out a little wine!

What did the left eye say to the right eye?
Between you and me, something smells!

How many skunks does it take to make a big stink?
Quite a phew!

What do you get when you cross a parrot with a centipede?
A walkie-talkie!

Why did the chicken cross the playground?
To get to the other slide!

What did the buffalo say to his kid when he dropped him off at school?
"Bison!"

What bird steals soap from the bath?
Robber ducks!

What do you call an alligator in a vest?
An investigator!

Why couldn't the teddy bear finish his dinner?
He was stuffed!

What woke the ghost up in the middle of the night?
Coffin!

Knock Knock!
Who's there?
Ice cream!
Ice cream who?
I scream every time I see a ghost!

Did you hear about the man who slept under a tractor?
He wanted to wake up oily in the morning!

What has four legs and goes "boo"?
A cow with a cold!

What happens when it rains cats and dogs?
You have to be careful not to step in a poodle!

Did you hear about the man who went to the doctor with rhubarb sticking out of each ear and custard up his nose?
The doctor told him to eat more sensibly!

Why did the woman run around her bed?
Because she was trying to catch up on her sleep!

What do you call a sheep with no legs?
A cloud!

What did the cat say when he lost his money?
"I'm paw!"

What do you get if you cross a llama with a tortoise?
A turtleneck sweater!

What game should you never, ever play with unicorns?
Leapfrog!

What did the big bucket say to the little bucket?
You look a little pail!

What did the left eye say to the right eye?
Between you and me, something smells!

How many skunks does it take to make a big stink?
Quite a phew!

What do you get when you cross a parrot with a centipede?
A walkie-talkie!

Why did the chicken cross the playground?
To get to the other slide!

What did the buffalo say to his kid when he dropped him off at school?
"Bison!"

What bird steals soap from the bath?
Robber ducks!

What do you call an alligator in a vest?
An investigator!

Why couldn't the teddy bear finish his dinner?
He was stuffed!

What woke the ghost up in the middle of the night?
Coffin!

Knock Knock!
Who's there?
Ice cream!
Ice cream who?
I scream every time I see a ghost!

Did you hear about the man who slept under a tractor?
He wanted to wake up oily in the morning!

What has four legs and goes "boo"?
A cow with a cold!

What happens when it rains cats and dogs?
You have to be careful not to step in a poodle!

Did you hear about the man who went to the doctor with rhubarb sticking out of each ear and custard up his nose?
The doctor told him to eat more sensibly!

Why did the woman run around her bed?
Because she was trying to catch up on her sleep!

What do you call a sheep with no legs?
A cloud!

What did the cat say when he lost his money?
"I'm paw!"

What do you get if you cross a llama with a tortoise?
A turtleneck sweater!

What game should you never, ever play with unicorns?
Leapfrog!

What did the big bucket say to the little bucket?
You look a little pail!